Casey

She's that kind of girl. When she walks into a room, the whole place just lights up, even when she ain't dressed up fit to kill. Even when she's dressed just like a cowboy, and working like one. When she walks in all the boys stand up straighter, or sit up in their saddles a little taller. Everyone gets real conscious o' how long it's been since he's shaved. And when she leaves, it's just like somebody took half the life out of a place.

Casey McFee was, indeed, that kind of girl. Not only that, but she could out-ride, out-rope and out-shoot any cowboy on the ranch.

But when Walt Granger decided he wanted her family's ranch, all of Casey's talents were not enough to help her father. Nor could she save herself from the crazed love of one of her father's deranged hands …

How would it all end?

Casey

BILLY HALL

NORTH SOMERSET COUNCIL	
1 2 0340594 2	
Cypher	06.09.02
W	£10.50

A Black Horse Western

ROBERT HALE · LONDON

ISBN 0 7090 7131 0

Robert Hale Limited
Clerkenwell House
Clerkenwell Green
London EC1R 0HT

Typeset by
Derek Doyle & Associates, Liverpool.
Printed and bound in Great Britain by
Antony Rowe Limited, Wiltshire

1

Dust hung in the high, thin air. The midday sun was hot, even though Ian knew if he rode into the shade it would be almost chilly. The mountains were like that. He sighed contentedly and yelled at the dozen or so cows with calves moving in front of him. They lumbered into a swaying trot for a short way in response to his yell, then dropped back into an ambling walk.

He could scarcely remember the Scottish Highlands of his childhood. He did remember the nostalgia with which his parents spoke of it. It couldn't have compared with this, though, no matter how great it was. Nothing in the world could match the feeling of being mounted on a good horse, moving his own cattle down out of the mountains to join his herd. He could think of nothing that even heaven could have that would be better than this.

'Aye, Lord, you've blessed me bonny,' he muttered. 'A fine wife, a bonny lass, a hale young

6 Casey

lad, and the finest bit o' land on earth to call me ranch. 'Tis nigh more'n a heart can hold.'

As he topped a small ridge he scanned the valley below him. Between three and four hundred head of stock grazed in the deep grass on this side of the creek. Though it was named Wood River, it was just a good-sized mountain stream. It teemed with trout. It babbled and sang with joy down the mountain. It watered the meadows and valleys. It gave the beaver places to build their dams and birth their young.

Several cowhands were spread out around the herd, keeping it bunched. From across the valley another rider emerged from a draw herding close to two dozen head of cows and calves, pushing them toward the bunch. The cattle Ian was hazing stopped as they came in sight of the herd. Their ears pitched forward. Their heads came up. They surveyed the herd, then picked up their pace, trotting down the hill to join their kin.

Ian reined his horse around and headed back up another draw, to scour it for livestock as well. As he found cattle, he would push them to the center of the draw, then ride on, keeping a mental count of how many head to account for as he returned from the head of the draw, driving all the livestock he had scoured from the brush ahead of him.

Half a mile up the slope the draw ended abruptly. A sheer cliff rose nearly a hundred feet. Where water spilled over the cliff after heavy rains or melting snows, it had worn a large round depression in the rock at the base of the cliff. The depression was filled with clear water, ice-cold even in the summer months. Ian guessed it was probably fifteen or twenty feet deep in the center. Two cows and one old bull lay in the grass at the edge of the water, contentedly chewing their cuds. A calf lay near each of the cows, stretched full length in the sun.

'Hey up there!' Ian called at them. 'On your feet, now. It's time to move. Hie on.'

The cows lumbered to their feet, eyeing him warily. The calves followed suit, running off a few steps, then looking back at their mothers as if waiting for instructions. The bull lay where he was, chewing his cud, glaring, daring the rancher to prod him out of his comfort.

Ian shook out several loops of his rope. Without making a loop, but with the hondo making a heavy tip, he began to whirl the rope. Instead of whirling it in a circle over his head, he whirled it vertically. It made an angry buzz as it whirled in a large, vertical circle. He nudged his horse toward the reluctant bull.

'Hie up there, bully boy,' he challenged. 'On your feet. Move it.'

The bull glared, unmoving. As Ian's horse reluctantly sidled nearer, he got close enough. The whirling rope, with the weighted knot on the end, seared across the hide of the bull's hind leg. He snorted. With each circle it made, the rope repeated the stinging blow.

After the third or fourth blow of the rope, the bull rumbled deep in his chest. He heaved his hindquarters into the air, then followed with his front legs. He shook his massive head, spewing a spray of saliva in all directions. He pawed the ground, and bellowed an answer to Ian's challenge.

Ian backed his horse a couple steps, keeping the rope whirling, but backing enough it no longer stung the bull with each whirl. The bull pawed the ground, eyeing both Ian and the whirling rope.

'Aye, you'd like to take me on a time or so, wouldn't ye, bully boy?' Ian laughed. 'But a little rope makes ye think another time er two, isn't it so? Now get ye movin' there.'

He nudged his horse forward again, bringing the whirling, menacing rope near enough for it to rap across the bull's tender nose. The bull emitted a sound that seemed half bellow, half squeal. He whirled and trotted off, shaking his head in anger and frustration. Saliva continued to fly from his mouth with each shake of his head. Ian chuckled and recoiled his rope. 'Aye. Nary horse nor bull can aye ignore the sting of a rope, though it ne'er breaks the hide. 'Tis a braw thing, to be sure.'

The cows dropped in behind the fleeing bull, trotting to keep up. Their calves ran, leaped and frolicked along as though it were all some great adventure.

Just as they broke out of the end of the draw,

where the herd would again come into view, a rifle-shot echoed across the valley and bounced off the mountains. It bounced back and forth more times than he could count, until it faded into the distance.

It was not unusual to hear a gunshot. It would be a routine matter if one of the hands decided to shoot a deer and skin it out, to provide the ranch with a respite from the steady diet of beef. It would be even more routine for any hand that saw either a wolf or a coyote to dispatch it summarily, if it were within range of his rifle. Only in camp, or back at the ranch, would the inquiries begin. 'Who fired the shot up in the aspen draw?'

Then whoever it was would relate what he had shot, or shot at. If he had missed, he would have to face a good bit of ribbing. If he had dispatched a predator, there would be a murmur of approval. If he had shot something exceptional, such as an elk or a moose, there would be plans laid to retrieve the meat before predators ravaged it.

What was it, then, that caused Ian to jerk his horse to a halt when the shot rang out? He sat stock still in the saddle. A strange chill shivered its way up his spine. He could have sworn his horse even shuddered. Ian swallowed. He lifted his broad-brimmed Stetson from his head, and mopped the sweat from his brow with his shirt-sleeve. He replaced the hat, staring intently at the top of the ridge, from where he thought the shot had come.

Even that was difficult to determine. The way sound echoed around in the mountain valleys, bouncing back from all sides, it could have come from anywhere. Yet, somehow, he knew with absolute certainty it had come from the next draw over.

' 'Twas nae just a shot, that one. 'Twas fell as the wail of a kelpie,' he muttered. He again fought down the urge to shudder as he lifted his reins and urged his horse up the hill.

Instead of dropping down into the next draw that reached like one of countless fingers from the valley back into the sides of the mountain, he stayed well up along the ridge. He rode slowly. He didn't even realize he rode with his huge, thick hand resting on the butt of his Colt .45. He was very much aware of the knot in his gut. His eyes darted back and forth, scouring the timber and brush ahead of and below him.

It was nearly half an hour before he spotted the horse. He recognized it at once. It was the best horse in the string of Red Sanders, one of Ian's hands. It stood in a small clearing, saddled, reins trailing on the ground. It appeared fidgety, but did not seem to be greatly alarmed, but it had been a good while since the shot.

'Somethin's happened to Red,' Ian muttered to his own mount.

Even then, the big Scotsman did not plunge down the hill. He kept his distance, quartering along high on the side of the ridge, studying the trees and brush below. He rode nearly a quarter-mile beyond Red's horse, then turned his horse around.

As he started back, his horse whinnied a shrill call. Red's horse answered from the spot where Ian had seen him.

He turned his horse toward the bottom of the deep draw. Shade from the dense timber closed around him. All the faint distant noises were shut away by the screening ridges and forest. In their place he could hear faint scuffing sounds of small animals and the fluttering of small birds.

Ian studied his horse's ears. They were forward, pointed directly toward Red's horse. His mount bobbed his head eagerly, anxious to greet the other horse. There was no indication from the animal of any presence besides that other horse.

But there had to be another presence. Ian fully knew it. Red was there somewhere. He would not be far from his horse. Red's scent, however, would be as familiar as his own to his horse. Maybe that was why he wasn't reacting.

Still, Ian moved slowly. He kept his horse in the deepest of the forest's shadows. He watched carefully in a full circle as he rode. It took him twenty minutes to reach the clearing where he had spotted Red's horse.

Even then he stayed in the timber. He sat his mount, studying the animal, the empty saddle, the surrounding terrain. Finally he slipped from the saddle, pulling his .30-30 from the leather scabbard as he did. He tied his reins in a knot and looped them over the high saddle horn. Then he stepped away from his mount.

The horse hesitated a brief moment. He looked around at his master, then back at Red's horse. Red's horse nickered softly. Ian's mount responded and walked into the clearing. Ian stood in the shadow of the trees, watching intently.

As his mount entered the clearing, the other animal saw him and nickered again. Ian's horse again answered, walking toward its fellow. Then, as suddenly as a shot, he shied sideways, snorting, his eyes fixed on a spot beyond the brush which Ian could not see.

As the horse spooked, Ian's rifle leaped to his shoulder. He watched the horse over the top of his gun barrel, waiting to see what had startled the animal.

The big gelding tossed his head, never taking his eyes from the spot he was watching, but which Ian could not see. He backed a couple steps. His nostrils flared. His ears laid back against his head, then pitched forward again. He tossed his head. Ian shrilled a short, sharp whistle. His horse immediately backed away from whatever he was frightened of, whirled, and trotted back to the rancher. Ian unknotted the reins and dropped them on the ground. 'Good boy, Buck,' he muttered.

He walked from the trees into the light of the clearing. He knew his horse. Without words, the animal had told him exactly what lay beyond the brush. His shoulders were already stooped beneath an invisible weight of loss and grief as he left the trees.

A dozen steps into the clearing lay the body of a man stretched full length on the ground. Ian knelt beside him, searching for signs of life. He already knew it was futile. A large pool of blood had soaked the ground beneath and around him. The small hole in his back looked almost benign. As he turned the body over, however, the exit wound of the bullet that had torn through his heart was a totally different story. Blood, bits of bone and pieces of tissue clung to the edges of a large hole in his leather vest.

'Shot 'im in the back,' Ian muttered. 'Shot 'im down like a coyote. An' him a fine hand an' a good man. Och, Casey, you'll be weepin' fer 'im, if I'm not mistook. I seen yer eyes a-dancin' whilst ye talked with 'im. 'Twas yin o' the things a father's not supposed to see, but nae father doesn't see. I could see the heart ye had for this lad, I could. And I'll be grieving a fine hand.'

He walked back to his horse and mounted. He shoved his rifle into the scabbard and reined the animal through the timber, up onto the far slope of the draw. He rode along the side of the ridge until he found a spot with a clear view of the clearing where Red had been shot. Then he dismounted and began to study the ground.

Within minutes he found what he was looking

for. Scuffs in the dirt betrayed where someone had crouched in wait. Looking about carefully, Ian spotted the brass from a spent cartridge. He picked it up and examined it. 'A .44-40,' he said, mostly to himself. 'Half the hands in the country have a .44-40. Including myself, some days, though I got the .30-30 today. 'Tis nae help atall, I'm afraid.'

He spent half an hour looking for any clear sign that would identify the assailant, but could find nothing more than bent grass, broken twigs, and scuff-marks in the dirt. He wasn't even sure in what direction the shooter had ridden away.

He sighed heavily. Returning to the bottom of the draw he heaved the body of the dead cowboy onto the long-suffering horse, still standing where his rider had been shot from the saddle. He tied the body in place. Then he led the death-laden animal toward the waiting herd.

2

Frying bacon sizzled in the huge skillet. Its scent drifted across two dozen bedrolls. One by one the bedrolls began to twitch, then wiggle, then disgorge cowboys in long underwear.

Almost as if following some timeless ritual, each cowboy threw back his blankets, sat up, and put on his hat. He pulled it down, twisted it back and forth a bit, adjusting it. Then he pulled on his boots, stood up, walked some two or three dozen steps away and emptied his bladder.

Then each returned to his blankets, pulled off his boots, and began to put on the rest of his clothes. When his clothes were on and properly adjusted, spurs were attached to the boots. A gun was produced from somewhere in the blankets and its loads checked. It was dropped into the holster and the strap secured to keep it from bouncing out.

Of the two dozen hands who turned out of their blankets, only one broke the routine of the ritual.

15

One young lad broke from his blankets, yelping and hopping as his bare feet encountered rocks or stickers, and relieved himself much closer to the bedding area than the rest.

One of the older hands called out to him. 'One o' these times you ain't gonna make it clear outa your bedroll, Nebraska.'

'Somebody oughta wake him up half an hour sooner'n everybody else,' another called. 'Then he'd have time to get fur 'nough away we don't have to smell his water all through breakfast.'

'Why'n't ya do that, Cookie?' another called to the cook. 'One o' these days he's gonna cut loose right in the middle o' all of us, then we're gonna have to chap 'im out.'

Nebraska ignored the comments, and hobbled carefully back to his blankets to dress. Within minutes the crew was seated on the ground around the chuck wagon, waiting for the cook of the roundup crew to set breakfast where they could begin to help themselves.

Using a long iron hook, the cook drug three large dutch ovens out of the coals of the fire. As he opened each, the smell of fresh biscuits mingled with the smell of the frying bacon. Without being asked, the cowboys began to grab plates. Busily frying potatoes in the grease of the bacon, the cook grumbled, 'If'n you boys'd wait five minutes I could get the rest o' this grub cooked afore you go an' eat it all up.'

Nobody bothered to answer his grousing. They

were too busy balancing their plates and the steaming cups of coffee poured from the large pot. In silence they hunkered down and gorged themselves on the hot food.

The food had nearly disappeared when Will, the big bear of a foreman, looked up and grunted:

'Lady in camp, boys.'

Every eye turned to follow his gaze. Still too far away for most of them to recognize, two riders trotted toward the group.

'That the boss?' a hand queried.

'That's Mr McFee all right,' Lance Sinclair replied. 'Him and Miss Casey.'

'How kin you tell that fur off?' the first hand marveled.

Lance's reply was spoken softly, but the intensity in his voice was unmistakable.

'I'd recognize Miss Casey as far away as I could see her,' he replied.

Will snorted. 'Forget it, Lance. She's way outa your class.'

Lance shot the foreman a withering glare, but did not answer. Another hand answered instead:

'She's plumb outa everyone's class. She's somethin', that girl is.'

A general murmur of agreement rippled through the assembled crew. It was again Will who responded:

'She is all o' that. That girl can out-ride, out-shoot and out-think every one o' you boys, an' have it done afore breakfast. If Ian had two o' her, we could can the whole crew of you boys. Now saddle up. Let's get some work done. You all know the lay o' the land. We'll just keep workin' up the valley, bringin' in everything outa the hills as we go. Lance, you an' Dusty stay down here with the herd today, an' spell Lefty an' Benjamin.'

'Another rider comin',' one of the hands offered.

As all eyes swivelled to the direction of his pointing finger, a pin-point of light flashed from the front of the approaching rider.

'Wearin' a badge,' Will offered. 'Must be the sheriff.'

Nobody asked why the sheriff would be riding all the way from Cody, out to the camp of a ranch involved in its annual roundup. The death of Red Sanders lay heavily on the mind of every hand on the place. They all wanted answers for his death, and so far none had even any logical guesses to offer. They had discussed, in quiet tones, every conceivable reason for someone to want him dead, and nobody could offer anything close to a reason anyone thought plausible.

Will interrupted the unspoken chorus of their questions. 'None o' you boys need to stand around an' wait. The boss'll take care o' talkin' to the sheriff. Hit the saddle.'

Wordlessly every man on the crew picked up his lariat and headed for the remuda, herded in close now by the nighthawks, and held in a loose bunch to allow each hand to rope the horse he would ride for the day. When every man was mounted, the

nighthawks would be free to turn their own horses
into the remuda, eat their breakfast, then turn
into their own blankets for much needed sleep.
They would sleep until early afternoon, unless one
or another of the hands thought of some sort of
devilment to play on them. It was almost always
the nighthawks who got a rattlesnake dropped
close to their blankets, then woke to somebody
yelling for them to look out. Or a skunk.

As he worked around the cook-fire, the cook
watched the other predictable entertainment that
was part of the morning routine. As each cowboy
saddled and mounted his horse, most of them
bucked a little, working out the kinks from their
muscles, demonstrating their displeasure at
having to work. Sometimes one or more of the
horses, especially those from the rough string,
would do more than the routine crow-hop that
was part of the standard morning wake-up regi-
men. In those instances, when the horse seriously
tried to dislodge his rider, the rest of the hands
would whoop and holler, reveling in the entertainment, offering bets as to whether horse or
rider would be victorious in the clash of wills.

By the time Ian and Casey rode into the camp,
the rest of the hands had been dispersed to their
assigned work.

'Git down an' grab a bite,' the cook called to
them. 'The boys left ya plenty o' grub.'

'Sheriff's comin',' Will advised.

Ian nodded. 'Aye. We spotted 'im. Ridin' with

the sun shinin' off his badge like he's darin' any man to take a shot at him.'

Will's eyebrows rose. 'Any reason someone'd wanta kill the sheriff?'

Ian shrugged. 'Don't know a reason any man'd want to kill Red Sanders, but someone did. Now the sheriff is comin' to look into it. If I was a murderin' man, I just might not be wantin' the man to do that, I'm thinkin'.'

'Red was a good man,' Casey offered. Her voice vibrated with emotion. 'I don't know any reason in the world anyone would kill him. He was so much better educated and refined than most cowboys.'

'I seen you was some sweet on 'im,' the foreman acknowledged. 'I'm plumb sorry.'

Casey looked away without answering. She dismounted from her horse, took a plate and filled it. She sat down cross-legged, leaned back against the wheel of the chuck wagon, and began to eat her breakfast in silence. The men took their cue from her actions and moved a-ways away, talking in quieter tones as they awaited the sheriff's arrival.

'Mornin', Sheriff,' Ian called out as the sheriff approached. 'Ye be in good time for a bite o' breakfast an' a cup o' hot coffee.'

'I was hopin' that'd be the case,' the sheriff responded as he stepped from the saddle. 'You'd be Ian McFee?'

'Aye. An' this is Will Handley, my foreman. Frog Martin is the cook. An' this is my bonny lass, Casey.'

As they were introduced, each stepped forward and shook hands with the sheriff. As he moved to fill his cup and plate, the sheriff spoke to Casey.

'Casey's an odd name for a pretty girl. The name would be Cassandra, I'm guessing.'

Casey nodded. 'Yes, but nobody'd know who you were talking about if you used it. I've been Casey since I can remember.'

'Never Cassie, huh?'

'Nope.'

'You know the boy that was shot?' the sheriff asked abruptly.

Her eyes clouded over instantly. She nodded. 'He was a good man,' she said softly.

'Was he courtin' you?'

Her eyes widened, but she offered no other indication of her surprise at his question. 'No. Not really. We . . . well, sort of, I guess. We spent some time together. I liked him a lot, but he wasn't actually courting me or anything. Why? What difference does that make?'

The sheriff shrugged. Without any apparent effort, he crossed his feet and sat down, cross-legged on the ground. Between bites he spoke to Ian.

'The hand you sent in to report the murder said he didn't know any reason anyone'd want to kill the man. Most o' the time, when nobody knows a reason, there's a woman involved somewhere.'

He turned his attention back to Casey. 'Anyone else on the place sweet on you?'

Will snorted. 'Is there anyone in the country that ain't sweet on that girl?' he asked.

Casey reddened, but held her silence. Ian answered the question.

' 'Tis a fact there's a dearth o' women in this country. Every hand on the place, an' every place for twenty miles, would fain court the lass if she smiled at 'em.'

'I don't doubt that fer a minute,' the sheriff agreed. 'Anyone doin' anything other than moonin' and wishin', though? Did Red have any fights about it with anyone?'

The three looked at each other for a long moment before anyone answered. It was Will who said:

'Not that I know anything about. I'd sure have noticed the marks, if they did. Hard to keep a good fight to yourself.'

'This isn't really about me, is it?' Casey pleaded. 'I mean, I don't want to be the reason someone gets killed! I wasn't serious about Red or anything. I'm not serious about anybody!'

The sheriff finished off his cup of coffee before he answered. With the back of his hand he wiped his moustache.

'No way to say, at this point,' he said slowly. 'But put your mind at ease. Nobody's holdin' you responsible. I questioned the hand your pa sent in purty close. He assured me you ain't no flirt, an' you don't try to get the hands to fight over you or nothin'. Some girls do that you know. Seem to feel plumb important if men are fightin' over 'em all the time. It don't sound like you're like that atall. If someone is fightin' over you, it ain't nothin' you kin help. Chances are that ain't it atall.'

'Then why?' Will asked abruptly.

The sheriff shrugged. 'If I knowed that, I wouldn'ta had to ride clear out here. I was hopin' to get here early enough to talk to your crew afore they spread out to work. Now I'm gonna have to ride all over this side o' the mountain, just to talk to all of 'em.'

'You'll be wantin' to talk to all of my men?' Ian asked.

The sheriff nodded. 'Never know which one of 'em saw somethin' or heard somethin' that'll let me know who wanted him dead. Bunkhouse and roundup camp-fire talk'll teach a man more o' what's goin' on in the country than a Pinkerton detective. I'll try not to keep any of 'em distracted from their work too long.'

Will offered, 'You'll be wantin' a different horse? I 'spect yours could stand a rest after ridin' 'im all the way out here.'

'I'd be much obliged,' the sheriff replied quickly.

Will walked a few steps away. He looked toward the herd, being held loosely by the hands he had assigned the task. He whistled sharply. When he saw one of those hands look his way, he motioned with his arm. The hand immediately turned his horse and kicked him into a lope, riding toward the foreman. As he approached, Lance Sinclair called, 'You want me, Will?'

'Yeah. Ride over to the remuda an' dab a rope on that big buckskin o' mine fer the sheriff. I thought you was workin' the cow herd today. Where's Burnett?'

Lance shrugged his broad, well-muscled shoulders. 'He said he'd a whole lot rather work the cows today, so I switched with 'im, and took his spot on the remuda. That OK?'

Will frowned, but shook his head. 'Yeah, I guess it don't matter. Anyway, get my buckskin fer the sheriff to ride today.' Lance's eyebrows lifted, but he voiced no questions. After only an instant's hesitation, he wheeled his horse and galloped away toward the remuda. He returned twenty minutes later leading a big buckskin gelding.

As the sheriff switched his saddle and gear to the fresh horse, Ian approached.

'I was nigh forgettin', Sheriff. I found this on the side o' the ridge above where Red was shot.'

He handed the sheriff the empty brass cartridge. The sheriff looked it over, then dropped it into his own pocket. 'It's a .40-40.' 44-40 of p 10

Ian nodded silently.

'I'd be obliged if you'd show me where he got shot, an' where you figure the shooter was. You buried the boy already, I assume.'

Ian nodded again. 'We buried him at the ranch.'

'He have any family?'

'He spoke of a family to Casey. He didn't speak the names of them, that she could remember. We sent a letter to the town in Kansas he spoke of, and addressed it to the parents or family of Red Sanders. 'Tis a sad thing to tell folks of the death of their child in such a way.'

'Better'n not tellin' 'em,' the sheriff offered.

'Aye. You'll be tellin' us who shot the boy?' Ian wondered.

'Not likely,' the sheriff confessed. 'Not unless someone saw or heard something they aren't talking about yet, anyway. We'll see. I ain't real optimistic, though.'

'Nor am I,' Ian agreed.

3

Excitement quivered in the air. It mingled with
the dust and the smell of hair-tonic, splashed
much too liberally on hair unaccustomed to its
presence. Groups of men and women stood about
the street of Meeteetse, Wyoming, visiting, laughing, and, occasionally, arguing.

'Well, get a load of Nebraska,' someone called.
'By golly, he cleaned up plumb good.'

'Warshed his neck, even, looks like,' another
agreed. 'Hey, Nebraska, where'd you get that silk
shirt?'

Nebraska grinned in response. 'Don't get jeal-
ous, boys. You can't all look as good as me. Just
watch and wish.'

'I'm watchin', but I ain't wishin',' another
responded. 'You forgot to button your britches.'

Nebraska's hand flew involuntarily to his fly.
Reassurance that he was, in fact, well buttoned,
did not keep his face from turning beet-red. His

eyes darted around in hopes no ladies had heard or seen.

'Cal Turner, I'll beat you to a pulp fer that!'

He was unable to maintain anger, though, in the face of everybody else's good-natured laughter. Attention abruptly veered to another topic. 'Did you see how big they're buildin' that church?'

All eyes turned to the framework of fresh lumber. ' 'Spect to have half the country comin' there, looks like,' another agreed.

'Gonna cost a bundle to build one that big.'

'That's why they're havin' this here box social.'

'An' dance.'

'Not the dance. Thet's different.'

'What's different about it?'

'Jist different. Thet there's a Meth'dist church.'

'So what?'

'So Meth'dists don't believe in dancin'.'

'They don't?'

'Nope.'

'Then how come they have a dance ta raise money to build it?'

'They don't. That's what I'm sayin'. The box social is fer the church. It an' the supper, an' the singin' an' such. Then along about dark, when the dance starts over at Swenson's barn, the church stuff is all done. All the money what gets raised from the box social goes to the church, but the church ain't got nothin' to do with the dance.'

'Then how come they're at the same time?'

'Cause if they don't have the dance too, there

won't be enough folks come to the box social. If not
enough folks come, it won't raise enough money to
git the church built.'

'That don't seem right to me.'

'Why not?'

'The church is usin' the dance they don't believe
in to raise money to build their church so's they
can preach agin dancin'.'

'Don't matter to me, long as we get to have it.'

'Have which, the dance or the box social?'

'Both. I don't never git no chance to eat with
some purty girl. I done been savin' up fer a couple
months.'

'Whose box you gonna buy?'

'How kin ya tell?'

'Watch 'em bring 'em! Why do you think we're
all standin' here watchin' everyone bring their
stuff?'

'You mean you watch to see what the box lunch
looks like that the girl you wanta eat with brings?'

'O' course, ya idiot! That's the way it's done.'

'Then why do they pretend nobody knows
whose is whose?'

'That's jist fer looks.'

'Naw, it ain't that simple.'

'Why not?'

'You think all them girls is thet stupid? They
don't never bring their own box in.'

'What d'ya mean?'

'I mean they all take their box lunch over to
someone else's place an' swap. Then they bring in

somebody's box, but you can't tell whose it is. You kin jist be plumb sure whatever box a girl brings in, it ain't hers.'

'Why, that's – that's – cheatin'!'

'Course it's cheatin'. But how else is Glenda Roberts gonna get someone to bid more'n five cents on her lunch?'

'Yeah, but think what'll happen if'n someone thinks they're biddin' on, say, Casey's, and they end up with Glenda's instead? Kin you imagine havin' ta eat a whole meal lookin' at them big horse teeth an' bug eyes o' Glenda's, when ya was all primed to eat with Casey?'

Commiserating groans went around the whole group.

'But what happens if some girl's got a steady beau? He ain't gonna be too keen on someone else eatin' with his girl, an' if he don't know what box is hers, thet's sure to happen.'

The self-styled expert looked around conspiratorially. 'That's just the point. See, Wilma Griffith, that I been seein', she already tol' me what her box looks like. That way it don't matter what box she carries in, I know which one's hers. All the girls that got a steady beau do that.'

'But what if somebody jist outbids thet feller?'

'He better not.'

'Why not? Ain't that what it's all about?'

'That's jist like tryin' to horn in on somebody else's wife, that's what it is. A fella jist can't let that happen, even if it costs his last cent.'

'But what if he ain't got enough money to keep biddin'?'

'An' somebody goes ahead an' outbids him? Why he'd jist plumb get whipped, if it was my girl! They ain't nothin' wrong with tellin' the fella biddin' agin ya that it's your girl's box. Then if he still tries to bid more money'n you got to bid, well, he's spoilin' fer a fight, that's all there is to it.'

A murmur from several directions at once diverted their attention from the conversation. As they turned, their eyes were drawn, along with every other eye in Meeteetse, to the four-seater buggy that had just arrived. Ian McFee stepped down from the driver's seat and offered his wife his hand. She dismounted from the buggy gracefully, responding to greetings from friends and acquaintances.

Then Ian offered his hand to Casey. An almost reverent hush descended on the crowd. The hush gave way to a collective sigh of admiration as Casey stepped from the buggy. Her reddish blonde hair cascaded to her shoulders in graceful curls. They rested on the shoulders of kelly-green dress that framed her breathtakingly beautiful face. The full figure usually hidden beneath the rough clothes of a ranch hand was accentuated by the lines of the dress. The ache drawn from the heart of every cowboy in town was a palpable thing. That ache found vent in audible groans from several directions.

'There's a girl most any cowboy would die for,'

an older rancher remarked to his wife.

'Or kill for,' his wife assented.

A friend standing by agreed. 'She is that kind of girl. When she walks into a room, the whole place just lights up. Even when she ain't all dressed up fit to kill, like that. Even when she's dressed just like a cowboy, and working like one. When she walks in, or even rides up out in the middle o' nowhere, everybody there just feels better, some-how. All the boys stand up straighter, or sit up in their saddle a little taller. Everyone gets real conscious o' how long it's been since he's shaved. And when she leaves, it's just like somebody took half the life out of a place. The sun even dims down a notch or two. You watch. Now that she's here, everyone will laugh a little louder, smile a little wider, just think that life is a whole lot better, somehow, than it was a little while ago. An' not one of 'em'll know it's 'cause Casey's here now.'

'Except the other girls,' the rancher's wife observed.

'They all do feel a little left out, all right,' her husband acknowledged. 'She's hard to compete with.'

'And she don't even know what she does to folks,' the friend suggested.

'I 'spect that's why she does it,' the rancher agreed. 'If it was deliberate, it wouldn't work.'

'It would be arrogance and conceit then,' his wife agreed. 'Look, nobody even noticed her brother get out of the buggy. He's a handsome lad, but it's like he doesn't even exist when Casey is around.'

Just then the church bell began to ring. Purchased even before it had a church or a bell-tower to hang in, the bell was suspended on a tripod in what would become the front yard of the church. The minister of the church rang the bell until the crowd assembled. He stood at the end of a long table, filled with carefully wrapped and brightly decorated boxes. Each box, everyone knew, held two lunches – one for the single girl who had prepared it, and one for the lucky fellow who won the bidding for the privilege of sharing the lunch, and her company, while they ate.

It was just as obvious that there were a lot more single men there than there were box lunches.

'All right, ladies and gents,' the minister began, 'you all know what we're here for, and you fellows have all done your best to divine whose box lunches all of these are, so let's start the bidding. Remember, be generous, knowing that your generosity will not only result in a most enjoyable and delicious meal, but in the advancement of the Lord's work as well. Cast your bread upon the waters, and it will return unto you fourfold. Now, what am I bid for this first box here?'

The bidding began spiritedly, and grew more frenzied as the number of boxes decreased. The box that Casey had placed on the table brought an exorbitant price, and nobody knew until the bidding was finished that it actually belonged to Glenda Roberts. Two cowboys, who both made it clear they thought the box they were bidding against each other for was actually Casey's, bid themselves clear out of money. They would have come to blows over the issue, except for the intervention of several men around them. They finally agreed that both would pay the highest bid they had money for, and to share the privilege of eating with its owner.

The last box to be auctioned off was the one Glenda Roberts had brought to the table. The minister was slightly hesitant to start the bidding. He was rescued from the dilemma immediately, however, by a generous bid called from the crowd.

Visibly relieved, he ran the bid up a-ways, then declared it sold to the one who had begun the bidding. Then he was as surprised as anyone to learn it was his son who had done the bidding.

The surprises of the day had just begun, however. The two cowboys who had been victorious in their bidding for the box Casey had placed on the table stood waiting with bubbling exuberance. Shyly, Glenda Roberts touched the arm of one of the men.

'That's my box,' she said. 'Thank you two for buying it. I guess I'm the only girl here that gets to eat with two men. But I put in a lot of food, so there'll be plenty.'

As if controlled by the same hidden string, the

two cowboys shot a glance toward Casey, then back to Glenda. Though hard-pressed to disguise their chagrin, their chivalry rose to the challenge.

'I sorta thought it was yours,' one of them lied. 'You bein' a friend o' Casey's an' all. When Casey brung it in, I just knowed it must be yours. I'm Joe Salter. I work fer the Rafter R. This here's Ralph Lauder. He works there too. We done seen you around, a time or two.'

The Methodist minister's son watched the exchange in obvious confusion. He turned to find Casey standing beside him. She put a hand on his arm.

'That was a fine thing to do,' she smiled. 'I hate to disappoint you, but that's my box you bid on, when you thought it was Glenda's.'

'What? It is? Oh! Well. All right! You're right. I am surprised. But what a wonderful and pleasant surprise! The Lord does reward those who do good, doesn't he? I – I just didn't want Glenda to be embarrassed, you know, to have nobody bid on her box would be humiliating, or to have it go for fifty cents or something.'

'You're Walter McBirney, aren't you?'

'What? Oh, yes. Oh, dear me. I'm sorry. I'm afraid I got rather flustered, and forgot my manners. Yes. I'm Walt McBirney. My father is the minister here.'

'Have you been here long? I heard some people say who you were, but I don't remember seeing you before.'

'Actually I only arrived a couple weeks ago. I just completed my studies at William and Mary College. I hope to be ordained to the ministry as soon as I find a suitable parish to minister to.'

They found a place to sit, beneath a large cottonwood tree, where they ate the lunch she had prepared. Neither noticed the eyes that watched from the shadows, or the fists that clenched and unclenched as they laughed and chatted together.

Walt was delightful to talk with. He had as broad a knowledge of things as anyone Casey had visited with for a long time. They talked of national politics, of the move to make the Yellowstone area into a national park, then moved to several literary themes. They discussed philosophy and religion and Wyoming weather, in no particular order.

It seemed to both of them as if they had barely sat down together when the strains of a trio of fiddles began to drift from the Swensons' barn at the edge of town.

'Sounds like it's time for the dance to begin already,' Walt observed.

'Already?' Casey lamented. 'But I've so much enjoyed our visit. It seems like we just sat down.'

'It truly does,' Walt agreed. 'Might I stop by and visit with you again, some time?'

'But of course! I'd love that. But aren't you going to the dance? You do have the right to every other dance with me, you know. I think that's the only connection the church would agree to, between the box social and the dance.'

'I am truly honored by that privilege,' he apologized, 'but I'm afraid my convictions and the tenets of my church rather debar me from that activity. I'm very sure you won't want for offers of a dancing partner, though.'

She laughed merrily. 'You're probably right, and my feet will be walked on more than the floorboards. But thank you for a most enjoyable visit.'

'The pleasure is all mine.'

He might have been right. There was certainly no pleasure in the eyes that marked his departure.

4

Nebraska reined in his horse and stood in his stirrups. A flock of magpies rose and descended just over the top of the rise. He scratched his head, then cringed.

'I sure shouldn'ta tied one on last night,' he moaned to himself. 'My head feels like someone's bangin' on it with a hammer. Now whatd'ya s'pose them magpies has got?'

He watched the birds for a long moment, then sighed heavily. 'Will's already gonna ream me out fer showin' up late, an' durin' roundup to boot. Just as well be a little later, I 'spect.'

He reined his horse that way and kicked him into a ground-eating trot. As he topped the low rise he reined in hard. He swore softly. 'Somebody done got hisself drug to death,' he muttered.

A scant hundred yards from him a saddled horse stood, reins dragging. The horse's head hung as if exhausted. Behind him a shapeless bundle lay motionless on the ground. Nebraska nudged his horse back into a trot. As he neared the other horse, he began to croon softly:

'Easy there, girl. That's a good ol' mare. No sense gettin' spooked again. Steady does it.'

The horse scarcely seemed to notice him. Twice she shot a glance back at the bundle behind her and tossed her head, but she did not offer to move. Nebraska rode up beside her and grabbed the trailing reins. Then he stepped from the saddle, gripping the reins tightly.

Holding the reins of the mare, he reached for the rope secured to the saddle horn. 'Hard dallied,' he said softly. 'Now why would someone hard-dally his rope?'

He undid the lariat and let the end drop on the ground. With the horse untied from the trailing bundle, he dropped the reins and walked slowly to what he knew he would find. He was not mistaken. Within the torn and wadded clothing was the battered body of a man. The lariat was wrapped and tangled around one ankle.

'Now how in Sam Hill did he get tangled up that way?' Nebraska marveled.

He turned the man over so he could see his face. He let out a soft groan. 'It's that preacher's kid,' he said aloud. 'Now what's he doin' out here playin' cowboy an' gettin' hisself killed?'

He turned the body this way and that, studying the scrapes and bruises. 'That blow on his head done killed him, I betcha,' Nebraska breathed. 'It's pushed plumb in. Odd, though. It's pushed in from the top, an' he's a-gettin' drug by a foot. How's a rock gonna hit him like that?'

He squatted on his haunches, staring back at the trail the mare had left. 'His clothes is tore up some, but they ain't bloody,' he mused. 'Only other man I ever seen drug to death plumb soaked his clothes with blood. How'd this guy get tore up like that without bleedin' none? Unless he was already dead afore he started bein' drug.'

Finally he nodded, as if making some sort of decision. He led the mare back beside the body and dropped the reins. Then he watched the mare. His frown deepened. 'Look at that!' he muttered to himself. 'She's so gentle she ain't even spooked standin' aside a dead body. Now how'd a horse that gentle get stampeded enough to drag a man to death?'

He picked up the limp form of the dead man and muscled him across the saddle of the mare. The horse snorted and tossed her head, but made no effort to avoid the burden. Nebraska stooped and put his hands on his knees, breathing hard. 'Glad you was a lightweight,' he told the dead man. 'Glad your mare ain't spooky, too. Never knowed how hard it was to hoist a dead man onto a saddle.'

When he caught his breath, he roped the body in place. Then he mounted his own horse. Taking the reins of the dead man's mount in his hand, he began slowly to retrace the horse's trail toward town. He was no more than 300 yards along that trail when he jerked his horse to a stop. He stepped off and studied the ground, walking as he looked.

'Would you look at that!' he marveled. 'Someone was leadin' that mare! Run 'er far enough to make sure he was dead, then veered off and rode that-away. Couldn't even spook her enough to get her to run, so he led her an' ran with 'er.'

He shoved his hat to the back of his head. He scratched the top of his head absently. 'Naw. I don't 'spect he even did that,' he corrected himself. 'He just run her far enough to make it look like he was drug. Whoever done it hit him over the head with somethin' an' killed 'im, then wrapped that rope around his ankle. Well, looks like I got me two right tough jobs to do. First one is to take this boy to his parents an' tell 'em he's dead. Then I gotta tell Will, so's he can send someone clear over to Cody to fetch the sheriff.'

Two days later he was still wishing he didn't have to do either one. It was the hardest thing Nebraska had ever done, hauling that dead body to town and telling his parents where he had found him. He could not explain why he didn't mention his conviction the man had been murdered. He just felt certain he ought to keep that to himself.

It was like the lifting of some great burden when the sheriff arrived at the roundup camp. The intervening two days had seemed a lifetime to him. The sheriff had scarcely dismounted when Nebraska approached him.

'Sheriff?'

'Yup.'

'I'm Nebraska.'

'You're the one found the dead man?'

'Yessir.'

'You sent a message it was no accident. Why?'

Briefly Nebraska recounted his findings. The sheriff listened silently.

'That it?' he asked when it was evident the cowboy had run down.

'That's about it, I guess.'

'Did you tell the parson?'

'Nope. Ain't told nobody, 'ceptin' Will. Figgered he had to know, to send the message to you.'

'Why not?'

Nebraska shrugged. 'Don't rightly know. Just didn't seem the thing to do. Whoever done it tried real hard to make it seem accidental. Didn't think I oughta tip my hand that I knowed otherwise. Leastways not till I talked to you.'

'Probably good thinking. Better to say too little than too much. Did he have any enemies you know of?'

'I didn't hardly know 'im. Somebody at the box social tol' me who he was. He just come into the country two or three weeks ago. Lookin' to get ordained to the ministry, I heard.'

'That a fact? Followin' the ol' man's footsteps, huh?'

'I guess.'

'You didn't see him argue with anyone at the dance?'

'He didn't go to the dance.'

'He didn't?'

'Nope. Could've. He went an' ended up with Miss Casey's box at the box social. Didn't know it was hers when he bid on it, o' course. But he ate with her, then she went to the dance by herself. He don't bel ... I mean, he didn't believe in dancin'. None of us was too sorry. Thataway, Miss Casey, she danced every dance with a different fella, an' a lot more of us got to dance with her than woulda if he'da got ever' other dance like he oughter've.'

'So she danced every dance all night? And danced with a different cowboy every dance?'

'Yup. She always does. Won't hardly never dance with the same fella twice, till she's danced with everybody what wants to once. Not just cowboys, though. Cowboys, farmers, homesteaders, stable hands, it don't matter none to Casey. She dances an' laughs an' makes everyone in a hundred yards feel like he's the most special fella in the world. They all leave there as happy as a buzzard in the plague.'

The sheriff snorted. 'Not the best comparison I ever heard, but I get the picture. Has it rained any?'

'Nary a drop. Ain't even had a heavy dew fer two weeks.'

'Want to show me where you found him, and where you found the other tracks?'

'Glad to. I sure want this offa my back.'

'Why do you feel it's on your back?'

' 'Cause I found 'im, that's why. An' 'cause I'm the only one what knows it wasn't no accident. I'm just a cowboy. I ain't no lawman. I don't like walkin' around with that kinda stuff in my head.'

'From what you've told me, you're more than just a fair tracker.'

'I am that,' Nebraska agreed. 'Better'n anyone around 'cept the Indians.'

'How's Ian fixed for hands?' the sheriff asked abruptly.

'Short,' Nebraska answered at once. 'If it wasn't for him an' Miss Casey doin' the work o' half a dozen hands, we wouldn't get roundup done anywheres close to decent time to do the brandin'.'

'Does that strike you as odd?'

'Why should it? Most places are short this year.'

'But why? And especially, why Ian. From what I hear, that girl of his draws cowboys like a dead cow draws flies. They tell me he's had a line of cowboys wantin' to ride for him, for nothin' if they have to, just in hopes she'll take a shine to 'em.'

'Yeah, that's a fact all right.'

'Then how come they're not there this year?'

'Hadn't thought about it. Now that you mention it, Ian ain't hired a new man all spring. I ain't seen nobody ride onto the place lookin' fer a job.'

'Ever hear of Yellowstone?'

'O' course! Everybody's rode over there a time er two. Strange place, with all them hot springs an' boilin' mud pits an' water spouts an' all. The Indians thought it was some sacred spot, or somethin'. I kin sure see why.'

'Heard anything else about it?'

'What else?'

'Anything.'

'No idea what you're drivin' at, Sheriff. No, I ain't heard nothin' about it atall. Why?'

'Just askin'. Show me where you found the body.'

The sheriff reined his horse and waited for Nebraska to lead the way. He did, grumbling to himself, but knowing he would get no information from the sheriff until the sheriff chose to share it.

5

'Ian McFee?'

'Aye. An' who might you be?'

'Name's Jake Callahan. You hirin'?'

Ian looked the newcomer over carefully. He sat tall in the saddle. His broad shoulders sloped to powerful arms. His hands rested easily on his saddle horn. His clothing was normal cowboy attire. The battered hat hung low over both the back of his neck and his forehead, protecting him from the intensity of the Wyoming sun. The rolled-up sleeves of his shirt revealed the ever-present long underwear that felt good in the high-mountain mornings. His leather vest hung open. The worn leather chaps and high-heeled boots could have been worn by any of hundreds of cowboys riding for ranches up and down the Big Horn Mountain range.

Two things struck Ian as out of place, however. The .45 that hung on the man's hip was tied down for a fast draw, and showed wear both on the pistol grips and the holster, which was uncommon for a cowboy.

The other oddity was the man's icy-blue eyes. They were flat and cold, expressionless as a snake's. With an instinct he would never argue with, Ian knew he was either an outlaw or a gunman. Or both.

Ian was not a man easily intimidated, and he didn't know how to beat around the bush.

'Be you a cowboy, or a gun hand?' he asked.

The cold blue eyes danced suddenly with surprise and good humor. Callahan smiled tightly.

'You get to the point, don't you? I guess I've been both. I'm just lookin' to hire on as a cow hand, though. I ain't runnin' from the law, an' I ain't lookin' for trouble. I do need a job.'

Ian looked him over again. He especially noted the way he handled his horse. The animal obviously trusted him completely, and he never tightened the reins. He was well fed, well groomed and cared for.

'Fresh shod,' he observed.

Jake nodded. 'Had 'im shoed in Cody.'

'Cody is bein' a fair ways off. Where is it you be ridin' from?'

'Down by Powder River. Rode for Gants last. Heard you was short on hands up thisaway. Ain't much fer work down there. Been real dry. Most folks sold off part o' their herd, savin' grass an' water.'

'I heard that. Well, Frog'll be ringin' the dinner bell afore long. Bide a wee an' eat a bite with us. Will, my foreman, will be comin' in. 'Tis him' ll be hirin' you, if it's to be.'

'Much obliged,' Jake responded, touching the brim of his hat.

Just then the tones of a dinner-bell clamored from the chuck wagon. Frog had moved his wagon ahead of the herd. He guessed with the precision of long practice how far they would move by meal-time. That way, he could have it set up and ready at the closest spot to where most of the hands were working. Jake and Ian rode in together.

Ian called out to Will. 'Will, this be Jake Callahan. He is askin' if we can use another hand.'

Will eyed the stranger with unaccustomed cool-ness. There was no malice or challenge in his tone but he didn't mince words.

'We don't usually hire gun hands,' he said.

Jake laughed. 'I gathered that from Mr McFee. I'm sure not wantin' to hire out as a gun hand. I got nobody on my trail. Especially not the law. I just need a job, and I'm a first rate cow hand.'

'If you're so good, how come you ain't workin' somewheres? It's roundup time.'

'Pretty dry down around Powder River. Nobody's hirin'. Most are sellin' off cattle.'

'Heard that. Well, we can use a hand, that's for sure. I'll have the wrangler pick you out three or four horses for your string. He'll most likely start

Casey

you out with something from the rough string, so don't be surprised.'

Jake grinned. 'Never fails,' he agreed. 'Much obliged. I got most everythin' I own piled on this poor horse o' mine. Would you mind if I put most of it in the chuck wagon till we get back close to the bunkhouse?'

'Ask Cookie 'bout that,' Will evaded. 'Fine with me if he don't care.'

Other hands were drifting in and grabbing plates, eyeing the newcomer with frank curiosity. It was Nebraska who spoke up first.

'You hire on?'

Jake nodded. 'Just did. Name's Jake Callahan.'

Nebraska stuck out a hand and gripped Jake's firmly. 'I'm Nebraska. This here's . . .' He went around the crew and introduced them all.

As though there were nothing unusual about a woman among them, Nebraska introduced Casey as he came to her, working his way around the group. She stepped forward and shook his hand with the same iron grip Jake would have expected from any other cow hand. He worked to conceal his surprise.

Most of the crew stepped forward to shake Jake's hand as they were introduced. A couple just waved a knife or a fork in greeting, concentrating on wolfing down their plate of food. The only exception was Lance Sinclair. He eyed Jake with open suspicion, and barely acknowledged being introduced. As soon as he finished his plate of food, he walked to where Ian and Will were discussing the afternoon's duties.

'Pardon me, Will. Hate to butt in, but you didn't hire that fella, did you?'

'Well, yes. Why? Do you know him?'

Lance shook his head. 'No, but I know his kind. He ain't a cowboy. He's a gunman.'

'He looks the part all right,' Will agreed. 'But he's got the look of a cow hand as well. He says he's got no price on him, and nobody after him. I don't know any reason to doubt that. Do you?'

Lance shook his head again. 'No, I don't. But he's still a gunman. His eyes are so cold you could get chilblains just lookin' at 'em. I don't think it's a good idea, havin' a man like that on the place.'

'There ain't a hand on this place that doesn't pack a gun a good share o' the time, Lance. You included.'

'That's different. Packin' a gun an' bein' a gunman are two different things.'

'I'll grant that,' the foreman admitted, 'but that's not reason enough to refuse to hire him. Especially when we need help as bad as we do.'

'It's a mistake, Will. Me an' the boys will work extra hard if we have to. We don't want the Mill Iron to get the reputation of hirin' gun-slingers.'

'Hiring one man that knows how to use a gun is not being a haven for gun-slingers, Lance.'

'Well, it's the first step towards it.'

'What's your point?'

'Well, the point is, I don't like the idea of havin'

a man like that hangin' around where Miss Casey is. It ain't safe.'

It was Ian who responded. He laughed. 'Aye. 'Tis Casey you're worryin' of, is it? Take your ease, me lad. Take your ease. If 'twill make you feel better, I'll have the lass challenge him to a shooting match. If you know she can outshoot him, 'twill ease your mind. And I've no doubt the lass can do it.'

'It's not that!' Lance snapped. 'It's having a man of that character around her at all. We don't need help that bad.'

'What are you drivin' at, Lance?'

'I – well – I really didn't want to mention it. I don't want to raise any false fears, but I think Miss Casey is involved in the killings.'

'Casey? You think she done it?'

'Oh, no! No! Not at all. That's not what I meant at all. I mean, I think they may have been because of her.'

'What are you talkin' about, Lance?'

'Well, it's just that Red, the first guy killed, was . . . well, everybody knowed he was really sweet on Miss Casey. And she was some sweet on him too. We all saw how her eyes danced and sparkled when she was talkin' to him, and how she just happened to accidentally ride up to wherever he was workin' all the time, an' how they spent hours just talkin' and all.'

'Who is "we all?" Since when do the hands on this ranch have time to watch who Casey talks to and when?'

'Well, it was just common knowledge, that's all. Bunkhouse talk, you know. Anyway, him an' Miss Casey was sorta sweet on each other, an' then he comes up dead. Someone just shot 'im. Got 'im outa the way.'

'You think he was shot because Casey liked him?'

'Well, it fits. It makes sense. 'Specially since the other one. Right after that box social, when McBirney paid all that money to get Casey's box, an' they sat there, clear up till after the dance started, just talkin' an' laughin' and actin' like they was plumb crazy 'bout each other. They didn't even go over with the others for the singin' time. They just sat there talkin' an' gigglin', that whole time. Then afore mornin' he was dead too. I think someone just wants to make sure Miss Casey don't get the wrong. . . I mean the one he figgers is the wrong man.'

'That's crazy.'

'Is it, Will? Then, right after the second one gets killed, here comes this gunman, that just happens to want a job with Miss Casey's outfit. I'm tellin' you, Will, we best not have him on the place.'

Will's patience reached an end. 'I'll be decidin' who we need and who we don't,' he growled. 'I listened to your objections, an' I'm tellin' you the man's hired. Now get back to work or he'll be takin' your place.'

Lance glared at the foreman for a long moment, then whirled on his heel and strode to his horse. He rode out at a lope without looking back.

The rest of the hands all hung back and waited, just to watch Casey. Somehow, as though it were a bit of gossip telegraphed through the whole crew, they all seemed to know she had chosen to ride Teton, the big black stallion from her own 'rough string', Picking up the crew's interest, Jake watched as well.

Casey finished her meal and picked up her lariat. The remuda hawks moved the horse herd in close for the hands to catch their remounts for the second half of the day. Casey stood relaxed, the large loop of her lariat in her right hand, the rest of it coiled in her left. As the herd trotted by, she stepped forward, whirled the loop once and sent it unerringly in a high arc to settle over the head of the big stud. She jerked the slack out of the rope and spun sideways, bracing the rope across the front of her hips, one hand gripping it at her right hip and the other holding it a foot away from her body.

The horse did not challenge the rope. He stopped, tossed his head, then waited as the rest of the horses trotted on by, and the other hands roped the ones they would ride. Some of them, who knew their intended mounts were less co-operative, instead of catching it on the way by, mounted the horse they had been riding all morning and used that mount to catch its replacement.

Hand over hand, Casey hauled the stud to her. She talked to him, crooned softly, combed the burrs and tangles from his coat, and slipped a bridle on him. Then she removed the lariat from around his neck and left the reins to trail the ground.

She put the saddle blanket on, then another heavier pad, then the saddle. Jake marveled silently at the ease with which she tossed the heavy saddle onto the large animal's back.

With no hesitation, Casey cinched up the saddle, strapped her recoiled lariat into place, fed the far rein over the horse's neck, then leaped into the saddle, barely touching the stirrup until she was seated.

She hauled the horse's head around and headed out toward the edge of the valley. Jake thought the whole crew were holding their breath, waiting for what must come. They were not disappointed.

The stallion trotted about a dozen strides, then abruptly ducked his head between his front legs and exploded upward. He didn't crow-hop. He bucked. He pitched and twisted and sunfished, pounding the ground, snorting and squealing. Casey sat easily on the pitching beast, waving her hat with one hand and holding the reins with the other. On perfect balance, she moved with every twist and pitch of the wildly bucking steed. Above the stallion's squealing her voice carried in a shrill 'Yeeehaw! C'mon, Teton! Buck!'

The animal responded, and so did the crew, yelling and cheering: 'Ride 'im Casey! Show 'im who's boss!'

'Hook them spurs, girl!'

Then another voice broke in, carrying over the top of the cheering, hollering crew.

'Quit showin' off an get to work, lass!'

That last from Ian's stern voice. Casey heard it with perfect clarity. She clapped her hat back on her head and hauled up on the horse's reins.

'That's enough, Teton,' she yelled.

As she yelled it, she slapped him once with the braided quirt, looped on her right wrist. The horse responded at once. He tossed his head once and trotted off in the direction Casey guided him.

'Wee lass'll try that one time too many and I'll be pickin' her up from the ground,' Ian groused.

From what he had seen, Jake didn't think that would happen any time soon.

Excitement tingled the air until the dust reflected it into the lungs of four dozen ranch hands, from half a dozen ranches. Cows bawled incessantly for the calves they were barred from reaching. Half a dozen cowboys on quick cutting horses kept them hazed and herded away from the calves they never stopped trying to reach.

Their calves blatted answers to those plaintive maternal calls, frantic for the comfort of a mother's side and her warm moist teats. Another half-dozen cowboys were just as busy keeping them herded away from the cows. They were allowed to drift as far as they wanted in the opposite direction, but not to move toward the cows.

It was doubtful that either group of cowboys could have kept the cows and calves apart without the aid of four dogs that belonged to the ranch. Ian worked the dogs with an expertise that was astounding to watch. Two of the dogs were assigned to the herd of cows, and two to the calves. They ranged back and forth in the area between each herd and the branding-fires, turning back any that got past the cowboys. When they failed to see a cow or a calf that was about to break free, Ian would give a shrill whistle and call one of the dogs' names. That dog would instantly look toward the rancher, to see where he was pointing. Following the direction of the finger, the dog would sprint to intercept the wayward animal, sending it scuttling back to the herd.

Midway between the herd of cows and the herd of their calves, half a dozen well spaced fires burned with almost smokeless heat. At each fire a cluster of branding-irons lay with the business end of each in the hottest core of the coals.

Will Handley called out, 'I think all you other outfits' cows an' calves are cut out, so let's get to doin' 'em. Tomorrow an' the next day we'll do the other outfits' that are still here. Today, everything is Mill Iron. Start bringin' 'em in.'

Casey was the first to move. Designated by the foreman to be a roper, because she was one of the best hands with a lariat, she moved to the loosely bunched calves. She whirled her rope twice as her horse focused on a fleeing calf, and let it fly. As the loop settled over the head of the calf, her horse set all fours and began to back up. Casey jerked the slack out of the rope, securing it around the calf's neck.

The rope whirled the calf around, but did not jerk it from its feet.

Immediately Casey touched the rein to one side of her horse's neck and nudged him gently with her spur. The horse turned and headed slowly toward the nearest fire, dragging the reluctant calf in tow.

As the calf was dragged within reach of one of the waiting hands, standing on foot by the fire, he grabbed the seventy-pound animal. Lifting it by a flank, he threw it on its side. Kneeling quickly with his knee on the calf's neck, he loosened the loop and took it off. As soon as it was free, Casey hauled it in, reformed her loop, and headed after another calf.

The cowboy with a knee on the calf's neck grabbed the calf's top front leg and doubled it up, giving him a good grip to hold the animal. As he did, another cowboy flopped to a sitting position behind the calf. He grabbed the hock of the calf's top leg and shoved his boot against the bottom rear leg, just above the knee. Pushing the bottom leg forward and holding the top leg straight back, he stretched the calf into a helpless, supine position.

No sooner was the calf stretched than another hand approached with a branding iron, heated almost to red hot. He jammed the hot iron on the calf's hip. The calf bawled frantically, trying to kick out of the iron grip of the two who held him down. Smoke billowed from the burning hair and hide of his hip. Its acrid smell wafted across the scene, mixing with the smell of sweat and dust. Watching carefully, the one with the branding-iron kept it in place just long enough to make a permanently seared brand on the hide, without burning a hole through it.

He lifted the iron and held it at his side. With his free hand he brushed the brand vigorously, inspecting it to be sure it was a good clean brand. Nodding approval, he turned and walked back to the fire, replacing the branding-iron and taking another hot one, heading to the next calf that was ready.

As he left the calf, another, older hand squatted beside the helpless animal. Taking the calf's scrotum firmly in hand he sliced off the end of it, then fished the testicles into the open. Shaving at the sides of the cords attaching the testicles with his sharp knife, the cords gave way. He tossed the severed testicles into a bucket, from which they would later be retrieved, cleaned, and fried for the much anticipated annual 'mountain oyster' feed.

As soon as he finished, the two holding the calf released it, allowed it to scramble to its feet, and hazed it toward the herd of bawling cows. When it was half-way there, a cow broke from the bunch, running to intercept it. She snuffled the calf thoroughly, licking it all over. The calf lunged for her udder, sucking avidly, more for the reassurance and nearness of his mother than from any real hunger. After a couple minutes the cow turned and trotted away, her calf hurrying to stay tightly at her side.

By the time the calf was 'mothered up' and gone, another had been dragged to the branding-fire and the process at that site was repeated. It took scarcely two minutes for each calf, and the work continued with an almost monotonous precision. The same scene was repeated with the same rhythm at each of the carefully spaced branding-fires.

Ian was everywhere. He watched the brands, offering suggestions when they were not branded quite deeply enough, or when a small break appeared in the singed hide.

'Don't whack them cords off thataway,' he called to another hand. 'Scrape 'em gentle till they be partin', then they won't be bleedin' too much.'

'Tater,' he called to another, 'don't think ye need be draggin' them calves that fast. Let 'em keep their feet. 'Tis hard enough on 'em to lose their manhood an' get a brand in its place, without seein' how rough you can be treatin' 'em.'

Jake started out flanking and 'front ending' the calves, then switched with his work partner when he indicated he'd like a change. Then Will called to him.

'You a good hand with a rope, Callahan?'

'Better'n most,' Jake replied.

'Take a turn, then, and spell Nebraska. No sense wearin' out some o' the horses while the others stand around with their heads down.'

Nodding, Jake strode to his horse and mounted. Shaking out a loop, he advanced to the calves and dabbed a rope on one, hauling it to the fire he had just left. By the time he got there, his place at the fire had been filled by another hand to whom Will had assigned the job.

At noon, the dinner-bell from the chuck wagon gave them a break from the grueling routine. After they had eaten and drunk copious amounts of water, they resumed as they had been, until the sun was low on the western mountains.

Will called out, 'Call it a day, boys.'

'I ain't a boy, Will,' Casey responded immediately.

'Call it a day, boys an' girls,' Will corrected.

'I'm only one girl,' Casey objected again.

Will grinned. 'Call it a day, boys an' Casey,' he tried for the third time.

'Why do you always have to single me out, instead of just treating me like the rest of the hands?' Casey teased.

Will shook his head. 'Women!' he groused, feigning disgust. 'Can't make 'em happy no matter what you do. How many loops did you miss today, Casey?'

'Two.'

'Outa how many?'

'I don't know. Seventy-five, eighty maybe.'

'Not too bad. You wanta do somethin' asides rope tomorrow?'

Casey sighed. 'No, I guess not. I like to rope. And most of the guys get all uneasy havin' me workin' calves. The heifers are all right, but the bull calves are a whole different matter. They act like I'm doin' it to them if I castrate, and act all embarrassed if anyone else does when I'm there. It works better for me to just rope.'

'You still wish they'd just forget you're a girl, huh?'

'Oh, I don't know.'

'What? What's this? Am I hearin' right? Do I hear "Don't call me a girl, I'm just a cowboy Casey", sayin' she kind of likes the hands noticin' that she's really a girl?'

Casey's face reddened. 'Well, it is kind of nice, sometimes. Jake touched his hat every time he rode past me today, and it didn't even make me mad. I was – well, it was kind of nice, really.'

'Well, whatd'ya know!' the foreman marveled. 'Will wonders never cease! The new hand's pretty good, ain't he?'

'He's really good!'

'How many loops did he miss, after I sent 'im over to rope?'

'None.'

'Never missed a loop?'

'No! And one of my misses, the second one, was right after he got there. He was watching me, and I missed! It made me so mad!'

'He rag you about it?'

'No. He pretended he didn't notice, but I know

he did. At least I didn't miss another one the rest of the day.'

Abruptly she grew serious. 'What's he looking for, Will?'

'Who?'

'Jake. The new hand.'

'What makes you think he's looking for something?'

She shrugged. 'He just is. He watches everything and everybody. Never smiles. Never joins in on any of the banter. Just watches everybody and listens. He watches the ridges all around all the time. His eyes never stop. He's looking for something.'

'He make you nervous?'

She shook her head. 'No. That's just it. I don't feel uneasy around him at all. Even his horses don't. He's riding a horse that he's never ridden before, and the horse trusted him completely from the start. And it's not like he's doing something wrong, or thinking about doing something wrong. He doesn't act guilty or sneaky or anything. It's just like there's something he's looking for. I don't think I want to be it, if he is.'

'Why do you say that?'

'I just think he could be a very dangerous man.'

'But you're not afraid of him.'

'He's not dangerous to me. Or to you or Papa or the Mill Iron, I'm sure. But he is.'

'Smart girl, that one,' Will muttered to himself as he walked away. 'Just the sort of thing I was thinkin'. I sure would like to know what he's lookin' for too.'

Something in his gut told him he probably would, before long.

7

'Ye'll be goin' to the dance, will ye, Jake?'

Jake's eyebrows rose, but his expression did not change otherwise.

' 'Spect I should?'

'Nay, lad, I was nae askin' that ye should. I was just askin' if that be what ye had a mind to.'

'Oh. Well, no, I hadn't really planned to.'

'You're not the dancin' type?'

Jake grinned. 'Oh, I like to dance well enough. I just think it prob'ly wouldn't be too good an idea, just now.'

'Fearin' trouble, are ye?'

Jake watched the rancher closely as he answered: 'There's trouble in the air, for sure.'

'And why are ye sayin' that, lad?'

'Cowboys talk. From what I hear; there's been two men killed within the last month, for no reason anybody knows. Half the boys on this ranch suspect half the others, thinkin' it has somethin' to do with your daughter. I think it has nothin' to do with her, but that ain't cuttin' no ice with anyone. There's just trouble in the air.'

'And what is your thinkin' of the reason those two boys died?'

'I don't know. Might have to do with somethin' outside this area.'

'Have ye somethin' in mind?'

'Maybe. I can't say, though. Just a hunch.'

'A hunch ye'd be sharin' with me, perhaps?'

Jake shook his head. 'Not yet. I'll sure share it with you when the time comes, if I'm right.'

'Am I right in thinkin' that has a reason to do with why you're here?'

The expression, or, rather, the lack of expression, in Jake's flat blue eyes never changed.

'It could,' he evaded. 'How long has Sinclair been ridin' for you?'

'Lance? Why he's been here for nigh seven years. Good hand. Loyal to a fault, he is. Why have ye an interest in him?'

'Just wonderin' is all. He didn't seem too keen on me hirin' on.'

'Aye, he was set agin ye, nae doot aboot that. Has no love for ye, yet. Might be havin' to do with the lass. He's a bit protective of her, ye ken.'

'I sort of gathered that. Because she's your girl, or is he sweet on her?'

Ian shrugged. 'I've not been askin', but I've never seen him shinin' up to her, nor heard the lass mention his name. 'Tis my guess he still sees her as the bonny wee lass she was when he hired on, that needs a mite o' protectin' from all these rough cowboys.'

'And does she?'

Ian laughed easily. ' 'Tis my guess 'tis the cowboys that need to be protected. Their heads that need protecting if they was to try something with the lass, and their hearts if they do not.'

Jake chuckled. 'I 'spect you're right.'

'An' how long can I be countin' on your stayin' around?'

'I can't answer that. I would like to stay on, though, for now. I'll pull my weight on the ranch. I ain't never been no slouch. I do need the job. And I ride for the brand. Whatever turns out to be behind what's happenin', I stand or fall for the brand I ride for. You can count on me standin' behind ya.'

Ian studied him for a long moment. 'Then I'll be takin' ye at your word, an' trustin' ye to let me know what's on your mind when it's time.'

'Thanks,' Jake said simply.

' 'Twould be some comfort to me to know ye'd be at that dance, though.'

'Are you askin' me to go?'

'Aye. I guess I am that.'

'Then I'll go. If there's such a thing as you need me, and don't see me, let loose with that whistle I heard you signal your dogs with.'

It was Ian's turn to have his eyebrows shoot up. 'You're thinkin' I'm meself in some danger?'

Jake shrugged. 'Hard to say. Doubtful. Just

whistle if you need me.'

He walked away, leaving the rancher to frown after him.

It was late afternoon when Jake caught his first sight of the Quigleys' Rafter R ranch. The low log-and-stone house was nestled against the side of a beautiful mountain valley. It was separated by a hundred yards from the huge horse-barn and complex of corrals. Two bunkhouses were arranged in such a way that they formed a semi-circle, with the barn and corrals at one end, and the ranch house at the other. The ranch had its own blacksmith shop just past the corrals, making it the first place encountered upon entering the yard.

Behind the bunkhouses, at the end nearest the barn and corrals, a 'four-holer' stood—a long, solidly built outhouse that boasted four seats within. The outhouse for the ranch house stood a good ways behind the house, arranged so that intervening trees and a rock outcropping effectively shielded both the outhouse and the path from it to the house from the rest of the buildings. In most ways, it was arranged almost identically to the Mill Iron ranch yard.

Turning from the main road, Jake rode into the skirting timber and circled the house to its rear. A hundred feet or so beyond the outhouse, he stepped off his horse and tied it to a tree. Then he walked forward to the rock outcropping. He found a spot within it where he could sit with a clear view of the ranch yard and the front of the barn, while being nearly invisible. Once the sun was down, and the torches and lanterns set up around the yard became the only source of light, he knew he would be entirely invisible.

Almost at once others began to arrive. They came on horseback, in wagons and buckboard, and some in buggies that ran the gamut from shabby to elegant.

'This country's gettin' populated plumb thick,' Jake muttered to himself.

One buggy was parked where it obstructed his view. He quietly got up and moved to the edge of the yard. Watching to be sure he was unobserved, he climbed into the seat and clucked to the team. He moved it forward about thirty feet. He wound the lines around the handle of the brake again, just as they had been. Then he returned to his vantage point.

The strains from fiddlers and a couple accordions warming up announced that the dance was about to begin. Jake paid particular attention to Casey, and to the line of young men vying with one another to dance with her. The same scene was played out around nearly every young, single woman there, but it seemed to have a special level of intensity around Casey.

It was not surprising, then, that every fight that night erupted from that queue of young men waiting a turn to dance with the belle of the Mill Iron. It was right after one of those fights was broken up, only to move away from the ranch yard to get settled in the privacy of the timber, that Casey took a break from the dance. She walked across the yard, and sat down on a large rock within a stone's throw of Jake's hidden position. She unlaced her shoes and began massaging her feet.

Within minutes Lance approached, appearing as if from nowhere. 'You all right, Miss Casey?' he asked softly.

Casey lit up the area around her with a bright smile. 'Oh, yes. I'm fine, Lance. I just needed a little break to give my feet a rest.'

'The bottoms of 'em, or the tops?' Lance queried.

Casey laughed brightly. 'Both,' she replied with feeling. 'Dancing skills are not among the things most men are famous for.'

'Neither is common sense, or a girl's safety,' Lance replied.

'What do you mean?'

Lance leaned forward. 'Miss Casey, it ain't safe for you to be here. Do you know how many fights have started around you already tonight? One of these times, some of those fights are gonna end up in gun play, and you could get hurt. Killed even. There's just too many men of an unsavory sort here tonight. I wouldn't be surprised if that gunman your dad hired is skulking around somewhere.'

'What are you saying, Lance? Are you telling me I'm in danger? That someone is planning to harm me?'

'Well, yes. No. I mean, yes, I think you're in danger. No, I don't think anyone is plannin' to harm you, but it's just dangerous for you to be here.'

'Why, Lance! You're worried about me! That's really sweet of you, but I'm quite capable of looking after myself, you know.'

As she spoke, Casey began lacing up her shoes again. Lance looked away, obviously embarrassed by that act of her 'dressing' in front of him.

'I'm plumb serious, Miss Casey. You ought to let me take you home right now, afore something happens.'

'Lance! Are you serious?'

'Oh, yes, Miss Casey. I'm plumb serious. I even brung an extra horse, just in case I needed to get you outa here. He's all saddled an' ready. C'mon. We'd best just go.'

'Why, Lance Sinclair! I will do no such thing. I came here to dance, and visit, and enjoy myself. There's three hours of dancing left.'

'But it ain't safe, Miss Casey.'

'Oh, balderdash! I'm just as safe here as anywhere. Now go enjoy the dance, and let me do the same.'

'I can't do that, Miss Casey, I just got to take you home where it's safe.'

'Oh, there you are, Casey,' Will Turnstall, a young cowboy from the Rafter R called out as he approached. 'We were all wondering where you disappeared to. Am I interrupting anything?'

'Oh, no, Will. I just sneaked off here to give my feet a little rest. I'm ready to go back now.'

'But . . .' Lance tried to interrupt.

Casey ignored him completely.

Will grinned. 'Well, in that case, may I have the next dance? I been waitin' all evenin' just for a chance to get to dance with you.'

'Why, you most certainly may,' Casey replied. 'And you may escort me back over there, if you don't mind.'

She took hold of the young man's arm that he offered her. It was very obvious that he did not mind in the least. That was even more obvious as he walked back into the circle of light at the barn, with Casey McFee on his arm. Every eye in the place widened with wonder and envy. Both Will and Casey ignored the stares and stepped into the area cleared for dancing as the music started again.

Lance Sinclair stood rooted to the spot long after the music had resumed. Finally he shuffled off a ways, then stopped. He looked toward the barn for a long moment, then turned and walked swiftly in the other direction.

Jake watched as, from time to time, a couple would slip out from the lighted area and walk together into the timber around the ranch. Once, only minutes after one couple had disappeared, a burly rancher walked to the edge of the timber.

'Thelma Lou!'

After a moment of silence, a timid voice

responded from beyond the circle the lights could reach. 'Yes, Papa?'

'Thelma Lou, what are you doin' out here?'

Another silence hung heavily for several minutes. 'We, uh, me and Josh was just talkin', Papa. It's too noisy to talk inside. It's nice and quiet out here.'

'You best get back in here. Folks is gonna talk.'

'Oh, all right. I'll be back in just a little bit.'

'Right now, Thelma Lou! Josh Biddle you get Thelma Lou back in there right now, or you'll answer to me.'

'Yes sir, Mr Thorson. We're on the way.'

The rancher stood there watching and waiting until the couple emerged from the trees and rejoined the dance. Then he walked away, mumbling, 'More trouble'n a whole pack o' polecats. That girl's gonna make us the laughin' stock o' the county.'

It was nearly midnight when the dance finally broke up. Jake watched from his place of concealment until Ian, his wife, his son and Casey were in their buggy and headed home. Then he mounted his horse and followed, well out of sight, riding to the side of the trail.

Twice on that road he thought he heard another horse. Each time he reined in his mount and sat, listening. After a time, he shrugged and rode on, but he never lost the feeling that he was not alone in shadowing the buggy the McFees rode in.

8

The thundering hoofs of a running horse brought half a dozen people into the yard before the rider skidded his lathered animal to a stop in the yard. Sandy Culpepper, a young hand from the Rafter R, leaped from the horse and strode to where Ian, his wife, and Casey stood. The mount stood where he'd left his back. His head hung. His feet were spraddled wide. His breath came in great gulps.

Unasked, one of the crew, attracted by the rider's entrance, picked up the reins of the horse. He began to croon to him. 'C'mon, ol' boy. You're jist about to fall over dead, ain't ya? C'mon. Let's walk a ways, then we'll git ya a little drink o' water. Then we'll walk a mite more. Then we'll let ya drink a mite more. Then we'll start rubbin' ya down. I got some lin'ment out in the barn that'll sure help ya some. C'mon, girl.'

As he led the horse away, Sandy blurted, 'Mr McFee. Ma'am. They's been another one.'

'Settle yourself, lad,' Ian rumbled. 'Another what there's been?'

'Another dead man,' Sandy panted. 'Will Turnstall.'

Casey gasped at the man's name. Her hands flew to her mouth. Her eyes reflected both confusion and sorrow. She said nothing.

Sandy glanced at her when she gasped, but turned back to Ian immediately. 'It looks like a accident, but it ain't. Will, he was my best friend. He hadn't no call to even be up there. Even if he was, they ain't no way he coulda got all tangled up like that. Not by hisself.'

'Laddie!' Ian broke in. 'Slow it down a mite. Ye've run on so fast ye've lost me already. Start at the beginnin', and tell us what happened. 'Twas Will Turnstall, ye say?'

Sandy swallowed hard and bobbed his head. 'Yeah. It was Will. We was all wore out after the dance, an', well we'd all had a drink or two. We didn't none of us notice Will didn't come inta the bunkhouse. Not till mornin'. When the sun first came up, we seen 'im. It was old Turcheck what spotted him. He's always up afore dawn. Says his bones hurt too much to stay in his bunk any longer. Anyway, he hollers an' wakes everybody up. An' there was Will, just hangin' there. You could tell he was dead, the way his head was flopped over. Knowed his neck was busted, even afore we got there.'

'Got where, laddie?'

'To the barn. He was hangin' from the beam, above the hay-mow door. I mean the beam above the door. He was hangin' pertneart to the ground. Maybe a foot or two from the ground, his feet was.'

'He was hanged?'

'With the hay-lift rope. Big rope. Fer liftin' the hay, ya know. It was in the pulley, but it was aside the pulley wheel, so it couldn't slip or nothin'. An' it was sorta wrapped around Will's neck like it just got that way on a accident. But it wasn't no accident, Mr McFee.'

'Why do ye be so sure, laddie?'

Sandy took a deep breath. 'Well, he didn't have no call to be in the hay-mow, in the first place.'

'Ah, but laddie,' Ian broke in. 'There was a dance goin' on, was there not? 'Twould not be the first time a lad took a lassie up to the hay-mow for a bit of a tumble in the hay, now would it?'

'Papa!' Casey protested.

'Ian!' his wife remonstrated. 'There are ladies present.'

'Well,' Ian defended, 'I'm just sayin' what the possibilities be. 'Twould not be strange that he was there with a lassie. And if that be the case, 'twould not be strange if her father caught 'em there, and followed up a father's instinct. Or 'twould not be strange if Will heard someone coming, and thought it might be her father, and tried to leave by the mow door and got tangled in the rope.'

Sandy looked back and forth from Ian to his

wife to Casey and back to Ian. 'That don't make no sense,' he objected. 'Will didn't even dance with nobody but Miss Casey and Thelma Lou Thorson. An' old man Thorson was watchin' Thelma Lou so close he couldn'ta got her all the way to the hay mow without gettin' caught if he tried.'

Ian nodded. 'I did hear that Josh Biddle was some in fear of his life. Thorson was callin' his lass and Josh out of the brush so loud I think there was nobody at the dance not hearin' him.'

Sandy grinned for a fleeting minute, then his face dropped to its outrage and grief again.

'But that don't account fer what happened to Will. Someone kilt 'im. That's all there is to it.'

'And why is it ye nearly killed your horse to ride over here and tell me this?' Ian asked.

Sandy's eyes darted around the yard. His voice dropped to a lower, almost conspiratorial tone.

'They's a rumor goin' around that you got some range detective here, pretendin' to be a cowhand, but actually he's here investigatin' those other two murders. I need to talk to him 'bout this. Will, he was my best friend. I gotta know who killed 'im, an' how come.'

Ian sighed. ' 'Tis true I have a man working for me who has some appearance of that, but if he is, then I ken naught aboot it. The man hired out as a cowhand, and he's a fine one. I've no reason to think he's anything but what he says he is. And the sheriff has been here twice, and he's said nothing to me of sending anyone to do that. I'm sair grieved for ye losing your friend, but there's naught I can do for it, I'm afraid.'

Sandy visibly wilted. He swore. 'I was so sure them rumors was right, an' I could have someone git to the bottom o' this.'

He swore again. Then he suddenly remembered he was in the presence of ladies. 'Uh, oh! Uh, beggin' yore pardon, ladies. I plumb forgot my manners. Sorry. Well, I guess I'd jist as well ride on back, then.'

'Ye'll be needin' a fresh horse,' Ian observed. 'I'll have one of the lads put your saddle on one. But I'll ask ye to treat 'im a little kinder than ye treated your own whilst ye was getting here. Ye can bring him home and pick up your own when ye can.'

'Uh, yeah. OK. Much obliged, Mr McFee.'

He lifted a hand twice, as though about to say something. Then he let it drop to his side again. He turned and shuffled to the barn. He emerged five minutes later riding a Mill Iron horse. He lifted the horse to a trot and rode wordlessly from the yard.

He wheeled his horse suddenly and rode back to the rancher.

'Oh, Mr McFee. There's somethin' else. Mr Quigley wanted me to ask if you've had anyone tryin' to buy your ranch.'

Ian frowned. 'Buy ma ranch. Nay. Why would someone want to buy ma ranch?'

The cowboy shrugged. 'I ain't sure. Somethin'

about Yellowstone. There's a move afoot to make
it into what they call Yellowstone National Park.
Make it belong to the gov'ment. Anyway, some
folks think they'll be wantin' to buy land clear
out here to be part of it. That'd make the land
purty valuable. Walt Granger, from over at the
Flyin' W, he's been tryin' to get Mr Quigley to sell
him his ranch, 'cause he figgers it'll be worth a
sight more once the gov'ment decides to do that.
Anyway, he wanted me to ask if he's tried to buy
yours too.'

'Nay, lad. 'Tis the first I've heard of any of this.
Tell him I've not been offered, and I'd not sell an
acre of ma ranch to him or to the government, and
I'll fight the whole government if they tell me I
have to.'

'OK. I'll tell him.' He lifted a hand and rode out
of the yard.

He was scarcely out of the yard when Lance
Sinclair approached Ian.

'Mr McFee. Could I talk with you for a bit?'

Ian looked at his wife and daughter. They
looked back with expressions indicating no idea of
what Lance could want. Ian shrugged. He turned
and walked a few steps away to where Lance
waited. Casey and her mother turned and walked
back into the house.

'Mr. McFee, it's got to be Miss Casey again.'

'What are ye talkin' of, lad?'

'Turnstall. The guy that was killed.'

'You're saying the lad was killed?'

'Well, yeah. Sandy didn't have any doubt of that, did he? I mean, we were all standing there listening. It wasn't like I was prying or anything. But, yeah. He was sure he was murdered. And I know why.'

'Then you'd best be tellin' me, lad.'

'It was Miss Casey.'

'Ye said that, lad. But that's not tellin' me anything I'm needin' to know. What do you mean, it's Miss Casey?'

'The reason,' Lance insisted. 'Last night, at the dance, Will and Miss Casey were off somewhere together.'

Ian's face turned beet-red. 'Now just a minute, lad! Are ye standin' there tellin' me my lassie was slippin' away into the brush or the hay-mow with someone? I'll kill ye, lad! I'll tear the foul tongue out of your lyin' mouth and feed it to the kelpies! I'll . . . .'

Lance started backing away from the advancing rancher, both hands out in front of him.

'No! No! That's not what I'm saying at all! No! Miss Casey would never do something like that! No! I'm saying that she just went out to sit and rest her feet, and Will Turnstall went looking for her. When they came back in, they came back together, and her arm was through his, like they'd been for a walk together. That's all.'

Ian glowered at the sputtering cowboy. 'Then why are ye sayin' that's cause for a man to get killed?'

'It's – well, it's just that she was showing an interest in him. In Will. That's all. She just danced with everyone else. But with Will, she went for a walk, out in the yard. I'm tellin' ya, Mr McFee, there's someone that just won't let Miss Casey show interest in anybody. Everybody she shows interest in, comes up dead the next day.'

'All, that's nonsense, lad. Nonsense!'

'Is it? Think about it. Red Sanders made it plain to everyone he was sweet on Miss Casey. Then one night the two of them went for a long walk together after supper, here at the ranch. The very first time he was away from the ranch after that, someone shot him.'

He waited for Ian to say something, but the rancher waited in silence.

Lance continued: 'Then she ate with that preacher's kid at the box social, and spent all that time talkin' and laughin' with him. An' then he up an' asks her if he can call on her, and she says "yes". Then the next day he comes up dead, and it looks like an accident, but I don't think it was an accident. Nebraska, he don't think so neither. Neither does the sheriff, judging by the way he asked everyone on the place all them questions.'

He waited again, but Ian only glared in silence.

Once again he continued: 'Then last night at the dance she shows a special interest in Will Turnstall. Before morning, Will is dead. I'm tellin' ya, Mr McFee, somebody is determined not to let

Miss Casey have a beau.'

Ian continued to glare in silence for so long Lance began to fidget. Finally the big rancher rumbled:

'An' if there be any substance in what ye're tellin' me, and I'm not thinkin' there's any substance in it at all, but if there be substance to it, what is it ye think I'd best be doin' about it?'

Lance hesitated for a long moment. Then he blurted, 'Get her married. Make her marry somebody. Find somebody that likes her, who's a hard worker, who's been around enough years you know him well, who'll treat her good, and make her marry him. Once she's married, whoever's doin' this will see it didn't work, and he'll go away.'

Ian glared at the cowboy for nearly half a minute, then he exploded into a paroxysm of laughter.

'Ah, laddie, 'tis nothing ye know of women. Nothing! "Make her marry", he says. As if a man could make his lass do a thing of the kind! 'Tis not the auld country, lad. And if it were, 'tis Casey we're talkin' of, here. Ah, laddie, that's rich. Make her marry!'

The rancher turned and walked into the house, laughing aloud and muttering to himself.

Lance watched in helpless frustration until the rancher went inside and shut the door. Then he whirled and strode to the barn, muttering to himself as furiously as the rancher had been. But there was no laughter interspersed with his mumblings.

Neither he nor the rancher noticed Jake Callahan, lounging at the corner of the ranch house.

9

A soft tap on the back door interrupted the McFee family supper.

'Ian, somebody's knocking on the back door.'

'Nay, wife. Why would any man knock at the back door?'

'I heard it too, Papa,' Casey insisted.

'Me too, Pa,' Robert, her brother, agreed. 'Want me to go answer it?'

'Aye, then. Nay, bide ye there,' he changed his mind. 'All o' ye, bide where ye are.'

He rose from his chair and slipped the .45 Colt from the holster hanging on the chair's back. He thumbed back the hammer and held it out of sight beside his leg as he approached the door. He lifted the latch and swung the door open.

'Jake, it is,' Ian said. The surprise was evident in his voice. 'Now why is it ye're skulkin' about the back o' me house, an' tappin' soft?'

Jake glanced around. 'May I come in and talk with you, Mr McFee? I didn't want the rest of the hands to see me coming to the house.'

'And why is that, ma lad?'

'I'll be happy to explain it to you,' Jake assured. 'That's why I've come.'

'Well, come in and bide a wee and tell us then,' Ian responded.

The rancher stepped away from the door and Jake stepped in. As he did, he swept off his hat with one hand, while closing the door quickly with the other.

'I've got to say,' Ian scolded, 'that I'm not like to be fond of a lad that skulks aboot like a coyote in the tall grass.'

Jake nodded. 'I thought it best. I heard the conversation with the fella from the Rafter R. They's some things you need to know.'

Ian studied him hard for a long moment. He thumbed the hammer on his Colt, lowering it carefully. Then he lifted the hammer part-way and rotated the cylinder so the hammer was resting on the only empty chamber in the cylinder.

'Then come in an' bide a wee, like I said. We're havin' a bit o' tea, for we've eaten our supper. But there's food yet, if yui're hungry.'

'No. No, thanks. I'll eat with the crew shortly.'

'Then yui'll be havin' a cup of tea?'

'Well, yeah. Yeah, I'd like that. I don't drink tea much. Coffee, mostly.'

'Aye, 'tis the American drink, it seems,' Ian complained, 'but it never takes the place of a fine cup of tea at the end of a day. Does the things ye've need to tell me need privacy, or can we stay here with the family?'

'Oh, no. That's fine. It's nothing that . . . I mean, they're welcome to hear it. Everybody's gonna be knowin' it afore long anyway. You just need to be a jump ahead.'

Ian's wife set a steaming cup of tea before Jake, and resumed her seat. Ian replaced his pistol in its holster and sat down. He watched the cowboy carefully over the rim of his own cup as he sipped the hot liquid.

'I guess, first thing,' Jake began; 'I gotta apologize fer sorta lyin' to you.'

'Ah!' Ian interrupted. ' 'Twas my fear from the first day. Yui'll be on the run from the law.'

'No, no. I'm not on the run, and I'm not a range detective, like Rafter R seems to think.'

'Then what are ye?'

'Well, that's what I'm tryin' to git to. My name's Jake Callahan, like I said, but I ain't from down around Powder River. I jist rode through there on the way here, an' picked up enough about the area to make it convincin' that I was from there. I'm actually from west Texas.'

'Texas! 'Tis a far piece from here. Why are ye clear up here in Wyoming?'

'Well, it's kinda a long story. The part I guess ya got a right to know, is that my family's all gone. My folks, my sister, an' two brothers done got kilt.'

There was a small gasp from Casey as he said it, but no other reaction from anyone else. They all studied him carefully as he continued: 'My folks had a purty nice ranch. Not big, but nice. Anyhow, there was talk the railroad was fixin' to come through. When they come through, they'd buy up land fer a right o' way, an' pay top dollar fer it. One o' the other ranchers in the area started buyin' up ranches he was sure'd be in the right o' way, so's he could make a big profit from it when they did. The ones that didn't agree to sell to him, he run off.'

'Ah,' Ian breathed. 'And I'm thinking your family did not run off too easily.'

Jake shook his head. 'They stood their ground. Didn't do no good. T'other fella brung in a bunch o' gunmen, an' run roughshod over everyone what wouldn't sell. After they got roughed up and burnt out an' what have ya, they all sold. 'Cept my folks.'

'They still would not sell?'

'Nope. So Arvid – his name was Arvid Billingsworth – he jist had 'em all kilt. I was gone when they come. They jist rode inta the yard an' slaughtered my whole family. When I got back, they was all dead.'

'And what did ye do then, lad?'

'Found Arvid. And shot him. Didn't help none though. My family's still all dead.' There was a long awkward silence. Unconscious of what she was doing, Casey reached across the table and laid a hand on Jake's arm.

Finally, Ian said, 'An' why is that having to do with where we are, now?'

Jake took a deep breath and exhaled it slowly.

'A few months ago, a fella come inta the area down there, lookin' fer gun hands,' he said. 'I'm sorta known fer bein' a mite handy with a gun, an' he come an' talked to me. Said he needed some men that could take care of theirselves, 'cause he needed to buy up a lot o' land, and the folks on it might not all be willin' to sell.'

'And did he say why he was intending to buy all that land?'

Jake nodded. 'He figgers the gov'ment's gonna make some sorta national park thing outa the Yellowstone area.'

'Aye,' Ian agreed. 'That's known to be going to happen. But Yellowstone is a bonny way from here.'

'Not that far, the way gov'ments figger,' Jake disagreed. 'This fella says there's a move in Congress to make the whole area part o' that park. Buy up all the land that ain't gov'ment range a'ready, an' make it all a place the high an' mighty can' go to vacation an' such.'

'This far from the water-spouts and mud pots and such?'

Jake nodded. 'This fur an' even further. He figgers to make a wad o' money buyin' cheap an' sellin' high to the gov'ment.'

'And what if the government does not decide to do that?'

'He claims he's got influence enough with the gov'ment to make sure that won't happen.'

'Does he now? And just who is this man that tells ye he would force me from this land?'

'His name's Walt Granger. Has a ranch called the Flyin' W.'

Ian's jaw clamped. 'I know the man,' he said. 'His ranch is not too far from here, but we do not neighbor. I like not the man. I've run him off from ma place, I have. But the thought that he'd bring gunmen into the country to make a war is more than I can believe. He offered ye a job, lad?'

Jake nodded again. 'He offered me two hunnert a month, my ammunition, an' my keep.'

' 'Tis a lot of money!'

'It's gun-hand wages,' Jake agreed, 'not cow-poke's.'

'And ye turned him down?'

'You bet! It'll be a cold day in hell when I help someone do to someone else what Arvid done to my family. The more I thought about it, the madder it made me. I finally just up an' rode up here an' hired on, to see what was happenin', an' see if'n I could maybe do somethin' about it.'

'And what is it you intend to do, laddie?'

Jake shrugged, 'Depends on what you all decide to do. Ya need to let the other ranchers, an' the homesteaders too, know what's goin' on. Then ya need to organize 'em, so's ya kin fight this thing together, not one at a time. If ya try to fight one at a time, Granger's gunmen'll cut ya to pieces an' take one ranch at a time.'

'Oh, dear!' Casey interjected. 'And you rode all that way, just to make sure we didn't get our land taken away? That is so – so – heroic! Isn't it, Papa?'

Jake reddened, and Ian snorted.

Jake said, 'I wouldn't call it nothin' like heroic,' he demurred. 'I jist cain't sit by an' let somethin' happen to you an' your place.'

Casey's eyes shone and glistened as she gazed into Jake's. 'I'm glad you're here, whether Papa thinks we're in that much danger or not.'

Ian snorted again, glaring at his daughter. He brought his attention back to Jake.

'So what is it ye're tellin' me we ought to be doin', lad?'

Jake hesitated a long while before he answered. When he did, his voice was distant, contemplative.

'Well, I 'spect you ain't gonna do much to pertect your ranch or organize your neighbors neither one till you know what I'm tellin' ye is right. Best way to do that is ride over to Granger's place an' ask 'im. Ask 'im if he's fixin' to try to buy your place.'

It was Ian's turn to think for a time in silence. He stood up from the table and strode to the window. He stood there, hands clasped behind his back, staring out into the ranch yard. As he did, Jake and Casey talked together in quiet tones, waiting for the rancher to come to some decision.

Casey's mother finished her tea and set about clearing the table. Robert, too, left the table and went into another room.

Finally, Ian said, 'Aye, lad, 'tis the best thing to do, I'm thinking. Tomorrow I'll ride over to the Flying W and just ask the man.'

'I'll be ridin' with you,' Jake said. His voice was soft, but it left no room for discussion or dispute. He rose, said goodbye especially to Casey, and went to the back door. He opened it slightly and looked all around, then slipped out and closed it quietly.

10

'You ain't aimin' to jist ride right inta the yard, are ya?'

'Aye, laddie. 'Tis exactly what I intend to do. 'Tis not a neighborly thing to do elsewise, now is it?'

'This ain't exactly a neighborly thing we're in, if'n you ask me.'

' 'Tis what we will be finding out, lad. If it is as ye fear, we will still not skulk about and act as if we are lowlanders until we know.'

'Man could die findin' out.'

'Aye. Or we could be finding out that they are neighbors and 'tis but a rumor we've heard.'

Jake started to retort, but bit off his response. His eyes darted everywhere, but nothing seemed amiss. The yard of the Flying W was clean and neat. There were two large bunkhouses, the barn, corrals, and the main house. There was a forge, but it was outside rather than in a blacksmith shop as at the Mill Iron.

They were halfway across the yard when Walt

91

Granger walked out of the house. He walked down
the steps and stopped half a dozen paces into the
yard. Another man stayed about two paces to his
left. It was that other man whom Jake watched
the most closely.

The flat-topped hat with the string identified
the man as west Texas, even though Jake doubted
that Ian would know that. From it to the Mexican
rowels on his spurs, the man wore what could well
be considered a standard uniform of that area.
His Navy Colt was in a well-worn holster, tied
down low on his hip. His hand seemed always to
hover inches from it. His eyes were flat and hard,
unblinking. His mouth was a thin, straight line,
neither frowning nor smiling.

Walt Granger greeted the arrivals.

'Well, if it ain't Ian McFee! Haven't seen you in
a coon's age.'

'Aye,' Ian responded. His voice was affable, but
his eyes were hard. ' 'Tis a good bit since I've been
seeing ye. 'Tis a bit dry, to be sure.'

'Yeah, but not too bad,' Walt responded. 'Grass
seems to be doin' all right. What brings you over
here?'

Ian ignored the brushing aside of the usual
small talk, and the abruptness of the question. He
came to the point just as quickly.

' 'Tis a rumor I've been hearing, Mr Granger.
I've been hearing that you have a mind to buy up
the ranches aboot this land, and that including
ma own.'

Granger's eyes narrowed. The man at his left, obviously a gunman, tensed slightly. Jake moved his own hand closer to his holstered gun, grateful he had thought to remove its restraining strap before they approached the yard. He let his horse shift his feet enough to give him a clear path toward the gunman.

Granger said, 'Now where did you go hearin' that?'

' 'Tis no matter where I've heard it,' Ian said. ' 'Tis a matter of knowin' if 'tis true. Is it, now?'

Granger blinked once. He glanced sideways at his hired gunman. He grinned suddenly.

'Well now, that's about as direct as a man can get, ain't it? Yeah, as a matter of fact, I do plan to buy up all the land around here. And that would include yours, McFee. I'll pay you a fair price, of course. Be willin' to go as high as fifty cents an acre.'

Ian snorted. ' 'Tis a cold day in hell ye'll be buyin' a foot of my land, Mr Granger,' he said. 'And 'twould be fine advice for ye to not be ridin' anyplace near to it, as well. I ran ye from my land once, and I told ye then they'd carry ye from it if I found ye there again. I'm tellin' ye the same once again. 'Twill be a day of soft music and slow walking if I find ye there. Or any of the men ye've hired to help ye to be a mangy coyote, as though ye couldn't be low-life snake enough by yuirself.'

Granger's face turned livid. 'McFee, you've insulted me one time too many. You'll apologize

for that, or I'll drag you from the saddle and beat
an apology from you.'

'Nay, ye'll not do that,' Ian said. ''Tis not a day of
the year ye could do it, unless ye could fight with
the wind ye're full of. But ye'll not be havin' the
chance today.'

The Texan at Granger's side spoke for the first
time. His voice was soft, but dripped menace.

'Maybe ya didn't understand 'im. The boss said
to get off that horse, so he kin whup ya some.'

'I don't remember anyone askin' you, brush-
popper,' Jake responded. 'Go back to Texas where ya
belong. You're gonna get hurt up here in real man's
country.'

The gunman looked sharply at Jake, then without another word he grabbed his gun and his hand
streaked upward. His gun was nearly leveled when
Jake's gun roared. The gunman grunted and took a
step backward. A puzzled expression crossed his
face. A second report from Jake's pistol followed the
first so quickly it was hard to distinguish whether
it was two sounds or one prolonged one. The
gunman grunted again. His gun slipped from his
suddenly weak fingers. He took another step backward. He looked at Jake with a stare of incredulity.
His eyes began to glaze over. He took half a step
sideways, then collapsed into a heap.

Jake's gun had already swung to cover the
rancher before the gunman hit the ground. He
said nothing.

It was Ian who broke the heavy silence. ' 'Tis as

I was saying, Mr Granger. Yui'll not be welcome on Mill Iron range. Seein' ye there, or seein' any hand what rides for ye there, will be understood as wishin' to fight. And when a lad makes me know he is wishin' a fight, I'll not be disappointing him.'

Without waiting for an answer, he lifted his reins and wheeled his horse. Jake said, 'You'd best shuck off that gunbelt, Granger. I don't aim to get shot in the back.'

As the rancher unbuckled his gun Jake said, 'Hand it up here. And his gun too.'

The rancher complied, glaring murderously at him the whole time.

'I'll drop 'em a ways up the road,' Jake said. 'Far enough ya cain't backshoot me.'

Then he wheeled and touched his horse with his spurs. The horse lunged forward, then settled into a swift trot that would quickly allow him to catch up to the departing rancher.

' 'Tis the first shot of a bad war, I'm afeard,' Ian said as Jake rode alongside.

Jake dropped the guns and holster onto the road without slowing. 'He prob'ly wouldn'ta tipped his hand thataway if he hadn'ta had one of 'is gunmen right there.'

'Aye. And 'tis plain he was intending that I should not leave the place alive,' Ian agreed.

'You got to git your neighbors together an' let 'em know,' Jake insisted. 'Make a plan o' battle.'

'Aye. And we have the work to do as well. We'll not be letting the work with the cattle and the hay

slide for fear of what might come. 'Tis a ranch we
have to run.'

'Then keep your hands in threes,' Jake pleaded.
'One man alone is an easy mark. Even Granger's
gunmen will hesitate some if there's three
together. And make sure they know there might
be gunplay. Most cowboys are fair with a gun if
they know they have to be.'

Ian said very little until they reached the Mill
Iron. As they rode into the yard, Lance Sinclair
strode to meet them. They put their horses away,
and Jake walked to the bunkhouse. Lance stood
blocking Ian's path to the house.

'What happened, Mr McFee? Where did you and
that gunman go?'

' 'Tis not yuir place to be askin' my where-
abouts, now is it?' the rancher remonstrated. 'But
since ye're askin', ye can tell the rest o' the lads. I
want all of them to know we are in for a war, I am
fearing. We rode over to the Flying W, for rumors
I have been hearing of their wanting to take over
all the land in the area. The rumors are true. It
was Granger himself who told me so, and offered
me fifty cents to the acre for my ranch. It was the
choice that he gave me that I could sell it to him,
or he would kill me for it. If Jake had not been
with me, it is without me my horse would have
come home. Jake killed one of the gunmen
Granger has brought all the way from Texas to
back his hand. So tell the lads. All the work will
be done with three men together. Keep your eyes

open and your guns ready. 'Tis not in my ken what will happen next, but 'twill be a war, I'm afeard.'

It took Lance several heartbeats to get past his shock to answer. When he did, the direction of his logic took the rancher by surprise.

'Mr McFee, you have to get rid of Callahan. He's the one causing the trouble. Most likely he's the one they're really concerned about. If you get rid of him, they'll be reasonable, and you can deal with them. I'm sure of it. I'm also sure that the main reason Callahan is here is because of Miss Casey. I've seen him watching her, Mr McFee. The man is in love with her. I can tell it. And Miss Casey can't talk about anything else but him. It's "Jake this", and "Jake that", and "Isn't he so handsome?" and "My, he is so strong"! I'm telling you, Mr McFee, Miss Casey just isn't safe as long as that man's on the place!'

Ian studied his hand, blinking several times. 'Laddie, ye've got Miss Casey on the mind so much yuir not hearin' a thing I'm sayin'. 'Tis Jake that saved my life today. 'Tis Jake that let me know the thing that Granger has planned. 'Tis Jake that we're needing more than any hand on the ranch. And Casey is a big girl. She can hold her own agin any man. 'Tis time ye stopped worryin' about her, as though she were yuir own sister. But since ye seem determined to watch out for the lass, I'll give ye a mite of job with her. I'll be trustin' ye to make sure she does not leave the place without her pistol and her rifle both.'

Without waiting for an answer he wheeled and walked into the house.

He was much too far away to hear Lance mutter, 'That gunman has got to go.'

11

White, puffy clouds deepened the impossible blue of the Wyoming sky. High up in the mountains, the clouds obscured the tops of the peaks. ' 'Tis rainin' up high,' Ian commented.

Jake squinted at the clouds obscuring the tips of the range. 'If n ya can't see the tops, thet means it's rainin'?'

Ian shook his head. 'Nay, lad, not all the time. It depends on the type of the cloud and the day. 'Tis a good bit of fog on the high mountains, and a good many showers that come and go. Up there it may rain fit to drown a frog for twenty minutes, then the sun shines as though 'twouldnae know how to rain.'

Jake shook his head. 'Different country.'

' 'Tis not like 'twas in Texas, I'd guess.'

'Not much,' Jake admitted. 'Wind blows pert-neart all the time, down there. Hotter'n blazes in summer. Wind in the winter makes you feel like they ain't nothin' atween you'n the north pole but

99

a barbed wire fence. Lot's o' big thunderstorms in the summer, but you kin see 'em comin' fer hours afore they git there. Allays come outa the southwest. Well, pertneart allays.'

' 'Tis a flat land?'

'Yeah, it's purty flat, mostly. Till you git over in the breaks. Around where I was, it's purty flat. Low sorta rollin' hills. Great grass, though.'

'And if you were havin' a choice, lad, which would you choose to live in, there or here?'

'Oh, no contest!' Jake replied at once. 'This is the most beautiful country I've ever seen in my life. I already can't imagine livin' anywheres else.'

'You ain't seen winter yet,' Nebraska responded.

'Winter purty cold?'

'Cold ain't the word for it,' Nebraska answered. 'It gets so cold up here you don't dare drain out if you ain't got shelter. If you try, it'll freeze plumb solid. Makes a solid column of ice from you to the ground. Freezes you plumb to the ground. Hurts like fire bustin' the ice off of it then, it does.'

'Aw, I ain't buyin' that,' Jake rejected. 'It cain't freeze warm water that fast.'

. 'It's a fact,' Lefty Cantrell chimed in. 'Nebraska ain't stringin' ya a bit. Warm water freezes faster'n cold water, ya know. I swear it gets so cold ya can't spit. If ya do, the spit'll freeze the same way, an' you'll have this icicle hangin' off your lip. I've seen guys with half their lip tore off 'cause they just tried to jerk it off.'

Jake started to respond when a sudden tug at

his hat startled him. Almost instantly the flat report of a rifle reached their ears. 'Look out!' Jake cried out. 'Someone's shootin' at us. Git behind some cover!'

It took several heartbeats for the others to respond. Then they all dove from their horses, scrambling behind brush and rocks.

Jake bent low over his horse's neck and jammed the spurs into the animal's sides. He had seen a puff of smoke from a clump of trees a hundred yards to their right. Reining his horse first left, then right, then left again, he wove a zigzag path as he sprinted toward the hiding spot of the would-be assassin.

As he approached, he heard brush crashing deep into the stand of aspens. He surmised his attacker, expecting him to take cover with the others, was startled into flight by his sudden attack. Gambling and hoping he was right, he rode directly into the timber, letting the horse pick his way now, hugging the animal's neck, the saddle horn pressing into his stomach.

The stand of trees was no more than 200 yards thick at that point, and he burst into the sunlight on the far side unexpectedly. Expecting to be met by another rifle shot, he whipped his horse around back into the cover of the trees. There was no shot.

He stopped and slipped from the saddle. He moved cautiously to the edge of the trees and looked out at the rolling side of the hogback extending out from the mountain. Nothing moved. He stood watching for a long moment, then began walking along the edge of the trees.

In less than ten minutes he found what he was looking for. Tracks of a single horse left the aspen grove and led directly over the top of the hogback. He whistled for his horse. The animal came at once, and he stepped into the saddle.

'Let's take it a little slower now, fella,' he told his horse. 'Glad I had my own horse today. Let's see where that fella's headin'.'

He rode nervously, watching the tracks ahead, but watching the edge of every rim and every good-sized rock as well. He was almost sure that at some point his attacker would turn and set up another ambush. He didn't intend to be surprised twice on the same day.

The tracks he followed led over the top of the rise far enough to be out of sight of the aspen grove, then turned up toward the mountain. Jake frowned.

'Fixin' to set a trap, sure's anythin',' he muttered. 'Otherwise he'd head away from the mountain, where he could put more ground behind him.'

The tracks of the horse he followed indicated the man rode at a brisk trot. That, too, puzzled him. 'Now if he's tryin' to git away from me, how's come he ain't runnin' his horse none? An' if he's fixin' to set up a trap, how's come he ain't walkin', so's he can look around and see the best spot to do it? It's almost like he either don't know I'm here, or he's jist wantin' me to foller 'im, since he didn't drill me back there.'

The thought turned circles inside his head. He followed the tracks for more than half a mile, when he reined in abruptly.

'Now he's had a dozen perfect places to set up another ambush,' he told his horse, 'an' he ain't even looked at 'em. He's jist ridin', like he's jist wantin' me to foller 'im as fur's I'll foller 'im.'

Suddenly his head whipped around to the direction he had come. He swore. 'Jist gettin' me outa the way!' he scolded himself. 'He didn't manage to kill me outright, so he's tryin' to lead me outa the way!'

He whirled his horse and poked him with his spurs. The horse responded at once, returning the way they had come. Jake did not slow him when he approached the aspens again, but clung low on his neck, letting the horse pick his way through as rapidly as he would.

Just before he reached the other side of the trees, he reined in. He quartered along inside the trees, trying to see what lay beyond.

In fifteen minutes he found what he sought. Less than fifty yards from the trees, Ian, Nebraska and Lefty were braced by four men whose horses bore the Flying W brand. Even from this distance, Jake could see the tension in the way his friends sat their saddles. The four men from Granger's ranch were obviously gunmen. All

wore the same west Texas stamp as the man Jake
had killed in Granger's yard. The gunmen were
all facing directly away from where he sat his
horse. He slipped from his saddle and began to
walk directly toward them. By the time he was
halfway to the group, his friends had spotted his
approach, but none of them gave any indication.
'Good poker players,' Jake told himself silently.

By the time he was within fifty feet of them, he
could clearly hear one of the gunman addressing
Ian.

'You shoulda took the ol' man's offer,
Scotchman. Now they're jist gonna bury ya on this
land ya wouldn't sell. Then we'll see if your wife
an' daughter'd like to sell it. If not, they's ways o'
dealin' with them, too.'

A second gunman chimed in, 'Ways that's lots
more fun, as a matter o' fact. That daughter o'
yours is a real looker. I seen her a'ready. We may
hafta roll some dice to figger out who gets her an'
who gets stuck with your ol' lady.'

Ian's face turned livid, but he maintained his
control.

'You men have made asses of yourselves enough
for one day, I'm thinkin'. Now turn around and get
yourselves off my land or ye'll never see the state
of Texas again.'

The first gunman laughed quietly. 'Can you
beat that, boys? The stupid ol' coot actually thinks
he's got a chance against us. Well, Scotty boy, give
it a try if you think you kin get your gun outa the

holster afore I fill ya full o' holes.'

'Mind if I try?' Jake asked quietly.

The four gunmen stiffened as though struck with a jolt of electricity. Almost as one they each turned their heads to crane over their shoulders to see who was behind them. The one who was the obvious spokesman was the first to find his tongue. He slowly turned his horse to face Jake. Jake stood with his legs slightly apart, his hand next to the butt of his Navy Colt.

The gunman spoke. 'I thought you was outa the picture,' he said softly.

'Guess not,' Jake replied. He offered no other explanation for his presence.

He noticed the gunman's eyes flit to the trees behind him and scan across them, then come back to rest on him.

'You was sayin' somethin' about wantin' to ride off Mr McFee's range, I believe,' Jake prompted.

The gunman shook his head. While he talked, the other three gunmen exchanged looks. One of them turned his horse to face Jake, while the other two stayed as they were. Two fer them an' two fer me, Jake thought silently.

The gunman said, 'Naw, that ain't what ya heard at all. You shoulda stayed in Texas. We was sent over here to make sure you was outa the way, an' get rid of the Scotchman, so I guess we can jist go ahead an' do what we came fer.'

As he spoke, his hand grasped his gun and he started to draw. He didn't get the gun clear of the holster before Jake's gun roared. The impact of the bullet drove the gunman from his saddle.

Jake's second shot beat the echoes of the first. The second man who had turned to face him grunted and swayed in his saddle. His gun had cleared the holster, but was not yet lifted enough to bear on Jake, and it seemed suddenly too heavy for the gunman to force it to do so.

Jake swung his gun to the other two, whose guns were just clearing leather.

'Don't!' he barked.

The two stopped, with their guns almost ready to clear leather.

'Drop 'em,' Jake barked, 'or I'll drop ya both.'

As they hesitated, Jake noticed that Ian's gun was in his hand, leveled steadily at one of the two men. He didn't know when the rancher had drawn, but neither Nebraska nor Lefty had completely drawn their guns. The two cowboys sat, each with his gun half out of the holster. The two gunmen looked back and forth from Ian's steady gun to the one in Jake's hand. As if bidden by some silent voice, Lefty and Nebraska finished drawing their own guns.

One of the gunmen said, 'I'm droppin' it.'

'Slow'n easy,' Jake said.

The man slowly lifted the gun the remaining inch to clear his holster, extended it to one side, and let it drop to the ground.

'Me too,' the other man said.

He lifted his gun clear of the holster and

started to reach out to the side, then quickly swung the gun toward Ian. He wasn't nearly quick enough. Ian's and Jake's guns barked at the same exact moment, followed a split second later by the roaring of Lefty's and Nebraska's guns. The riddled body of the gunman flopped from the saddle, striking the ground before his gun did. His gun, freed from his grip by his sudden death, landed on his chest. It discharged as it struck him, driving yet another slug though his already dead body.

'Would you look at that!' Nebraska marveled. 'His own gun even shot 'im, after he was already dead.'

'That's bad, when a man's own gun shoots 'im all by itself,' Lefty agreed.

The surviving gunman looked around at the four men.

'Listen,' he said. His voice was half an octave too high and just a little too loud. 'Listen, I'm outa this fight. I'm headin' back to Texas. I'll – I'll take these boys' bodies back to Granger, if ya want me to, but then I'm outa here. I don't want no part of this. If you boys let me live, I promise ya, I'm outa this fight fer good.'

It was Ian who responded. 'Aye, lad, we'll take your word for that. You can put yuir friends across their saddles and tie them there. Then you can lead them back to Granger and tell him that Ian says, "Keep your men from my land or 'twill be you that'll be bein' led slowly home across your saddle". Tell him I said that. Then you hie on back to Texas, and thank the good Lord the whole way that ye can ride there of your own will.'

'Oh, I will, Mr McFee, I surely will. If you boys will jist help me load them onto their saddles, that's just exactly what I'll do. I surely will. And I thank you. I ain't never thanked a man fer my life afore, but I'm thankin' you. All four of you. I surely am.'

Half an hour later, the three gunmen were loaded onto horses that were carefully inspected for more weapons. A pile of guns and ammunition, gleaned from the four sets of saddle-bags, lay on the ground. The survivor of the four was only too glad to lead the string of horses with their macabre burdens off Mill Iron range.

12

'It wasn't the same bunch.'

Ian's eyebrows lifted in obvious disagreement. 'Nay, lad. 'Twas only tae lead ye off from the rest of us the man put a hole in your hat.'

Jake shook his head. 'No, he just overshot. The aspen grove was a lot higher'n where we was sittin' our horses. Shootin' downhill, thataway, it's easy to overshoot. If he was part o' the same outfit, he'da jist shot me an' got rid o' me anyway. They was fixin' to shoot all three o' ya when I came back.'

'Then why was the man leavin' such a trail?' Ian asked. 'And why was the man riding at a pace to only stay a wee bit ahead from you?'

'He wasn't. He didn't have any idea I was following him. He expected me to not find him in the trees, and figured I'd have better sense than to just follow him. That's an easy way to get bush-whacked, an' most everybody knows it. No, he figgered since I didn't ketch 'im in the trees, I'd jist turn around an' go back. The others heard the shot and I wasn't with you, so they just figured the shot had taken care of me. No, the one that shot at me was jist circlin' around, headin' back fer here.'

Ian's surprise was instant and obvious. 'Here? What are ye tellin' me, lad?'

'He was someone from Mill Iron.'

'Now how could ye be knowin' that? Did ye see the man?'

'Nay. I mean, no. Now see there! Ya even got me talkin' like a Scotchman.'

'Scotsman, lad. Not Scotchman,' Ian corrected him.

Jake frowned as though unable to distinguish the difference. Then he shrugged and continued as if he had not been interrupted. 'But I saw his tracks. Harry, your blacksmith, makes a horseshoe that's a mite different from any I ever seen. Thet horse was shod with a set of his horseshoes.'

'He was ridin' a Mill Iron horse?' Ian echoed in disbelief.

'Yup.'

'Now, lad, who on the Mill Iron would be trying to kill you?'

'The same one that killed Red an' the preacher's son, and Turnstall.'

Ian studied his hand carefully, but it was Casey who answered.

'Jake, do you know who it is?'

Jake looked at her carefully. As though making

a decision, he said, 'Who got the most upset when you'n me started ridin' off together sometimes, checkin' cows an' such?'

'Me!' Ian interjected at once. ' 'Till I was knowin' ye had honorable intentions, at least.'

Jake grinned. 'I sorta noticed that. I never got questioned so hard 'bout wantin' to take girl for a ride since I was sixteen years old.'

'And were ye having honest intentions then, lad?'

Jake turned red unexpectedly. 'I'd jist as soon not git inta thet,' he said. 'Carlita Martinez did not have an understanding father, and he did not trust sixteen-year-old boys.'

' 'Tis a smart father, I'm thinking.'

Jake turned the conversation back to its original subject. 'But who didn't like me ridin' with Casey? 'Specially when he figgered out she sure didn't mind bein' with me?'

'Lance,' Casey offered softly.

Jake nodded. He looked at Casey. 'He's the one what was most upset at you likin' Red some, too. Not to mention eatin' with the preacher fella at the box social. He was plumb hot about thet, from what I hear.'

Casey walked up directly in front of Jake and looked up into his eyes. He returned the look, feeling for all the world as if he were falling into their blue depths and sinking, sinking away from everything that surrounded them. He swallowed hard. She reached out both hands and rested them on his arms, just below the elbow. Fire spread from her touch and coursed through his whole system.

'It isn't really all because of me, is it? I don't want it to be because of me.'

Jake swallowed hard. Somehow he could not focus his thoughts. His head buzzed. He reached out both arms and took hold of her shoulders. He tried to answer, but his mouth was too dry to speak. He swallowed again.

Casey said, 'Oh, Jake? It is, isn't it? It's because of me!'

She sagged forward toward him. His arms slid around her shoulders as if it were the most natural thing in the world for him to do. He pulled her gently against him, and held her. She turned her face sideways and laid it against his chest. He tipped his head down and spoke softly into the intoxicating fragrance of her hair.

'It ain't noways your fault, Casey. You got no responsibility fer it. Someone on the ranch is jist head over heels in love with you, an' don't know what to do about it, 'cept to get rid o' anyone else he thinks you're interested in. I ain't sure it's Lance atall, but he's the first one I figger it is. I know he's plumb in love with ya. Thet's as plain as the nose on your face. An' I sure can't blame a man fer that. Fer bein' in love with you, I mean. I been plumb in love with you since the first day I seen ya. But thet ain't your fault neither.'

She moved slightly away from him but stayed

within the circle of his arms. She looked up into
his face. She studied him carefully, her eyes focus-
ing first on one of his eyes then the other. She
lifted a hand and stroked softly down the line of
his jaw, marveling at the coarseness of the stubble
of beard.

'Jake Callahan, do you mean that?'

'Mean what?'

'What you said.'

'That the fella what shot at me's from Mill Iron.
Yes ma'am.'

Her eyes flashed. 'That's not what I meant! The
other thing you said.'

Realization flashed across his eyes, replaced
instantly with a mischievous twinkle. 'Oh, the
other thing. That he thinks he's in love with you.
Yeah, I meant that too.'

She shoved at him roughly, but he kept his
arms around her, and she made no real effort to
escape his grip.

'If you don't say it again, I'm going to stomp on
your foot!' she threatened.

'Say what?'

'Say you love me, you Texas idiot!'

'Oh. Okay. You love me, you Texas idiot. There.
I said it.'

She stomped on his foot. He howled in surprise
and pain and jumped back, dancing on one foot
and holding the other one with both hands. Ian
roared with laughter.

'Aye! Now there's a just desert! Here's a lad

romancing ma own bonny lass right in front of ma face, just as though I'm not even existing. And she breaks the lad's toe, she does.'

'Well, he deserved it,' Casey defended.

'Aye, he did that,' Ian agreed. 'But it's putting aside the sweet talk we have to do. If 'tis true the man who killed the other two lads is here on me own ranch, and in love with me own lassie, whether 'tis Lance or not, he will be trying harder than ever if the twa of ye let be known ye be swearing feal.'

Jake gave Casey a long look. 'Swearin' feal,' he echoed. 'I like the ring o' thet. Ain't sure what it means, but it sounds good.'

Then he pried his eyes from hers and forced his attention to Ian.

'Thet ain't half of it,' he said. 'If'n Granger sent them boys over to kill ya, an' 'e did fer sure, thet means he's fixin' ta move on the rest o' the ranchers an' homesteaders. But he ain't gonna try to take 'em all on till he gits rid o' you. Thet means we kin expect the whole passel o' his hands an' all his hired gunmen to come swoopin' over here right fast.'

Incredulity swam in Ian's response. 'You're thinking they'll come like an army to just wipe us away? Nay, lad. Not even Walter Granger would try such a thing!'

'What's to stop him? By the time anyone could get word out to the authorities, we'll all be dead, if he kin make it work. Then who's gonna tell the authorities that you didn't really sign that deed to your place? Or that any o' the rest of the ranchers an' homesteaders didn't sign their land over to him? He'll have as many witnesses as he needs to swear we all sold out an' lit outa the country. They'll haul our bodies up to Yellowstone and throw 'em in one o' them mud pits or somethin', where they'll never be found, and nobody'll ever know what happened.'

Casey's face blanched as he talked. By the time he finished, her face and her father's were the same pasty shade of gray.

'Lad! What are ye sayin'?'

'Mr McFee, I ain't got time to say it twice. We gotta get movin' to be ready. We need to send some of the boys off to round up as many neighbors as we kin, an' have 'em come over here, loaded fer bear. We need to send one man off to Cody on a fast horse to git the sheriff. Tell 'im the whole story. Have 'im wire fer a US marshal, or even the army, if'n he kin. He won't be hard to convince. The sheriff knows Granger's up to somethin'. Thet's how's come he was askin' all them questions. He asked me about Yellowstone, an' he asked me about Granger, the very first time I seen him.'

Ian's brief period of incredulous disbelief passed and he began to show the mettle that had carved this ranch out of Wyoming wilderness. He strode to the yard and clanged the dinner-bell stridently. As men began appearing from the bunkhouse, the blacksmith, the barn, the corrals, he began to bark orders.

'Lefty, ye be ridin' to Rafter R and the homesteads ye can reach on the way there and back again. Tell them Granger is coming with all his crew and the gun hands he hired in Texas, to slaughter us all. 'Tis a full-scale range war, it is. He means to have all our land. Then ask, can they come lend a hand. Hie as quick as ye can. Snuffy, ye be ridin' to Meeteetse the same. Tater, ye be ridin' to the Slash M the same. Frog, ye be ridin' out and round up all our boys that are not in the yard, that ye can get back here in three hours. Will, ye be ridin' to Cody. Take a horse with good bottom in him, and if ye have to ride him to death, then do ye make sure he gets ye there before he dies.

'Tell the sheriff what is come. Tell him Walter Granger means to buy the whole country to resell it to the government, and kill us all to get it. Tell him we need the marshal or the army or all the men he can send us, though 'twill be over before he gets here, most like. 'Tis yuir being my foreman will make him listen to you right well. The rest of you, to the house and we will plan.'

He turned to find Jake and Casey standing behind him, their arms around one another.

'Lass,' he said, 'ye'll be bidin' at the house with your mother and Robert. Ye'll be shuttered in well, and ye know how to use the loopholes in the shutters. Ye've not seen attacks like we had from the Indians in the early days, but ye can shoot a fly from a horse's ear, and ye be knowin' how to defend the house. I'll be leavin' two men in the house with you, and we will be not far afield.'

'Leave Jake, Papa. Please?'

'Nay, lass. I cannae. I'm needing him too much. If we have not the surprise, and the best of our guns where the surprise is, we'll no last till the help comes.'

He turned to another of his hands. 'Nebraska, I've sent ma foreman away, so I'm asking ye to take charge of the rest of the yard. Ye'll be wantin' men in the hay-mow o' ma barn. The bunkhouse is made to defend. Ye'll be closin' the shutters and finding the loopholes. Ye've got a good field of fire, ye have, from them. If ye've men on each side, ye can cover a good bit and the shutters are thick enough to stop a bullet. Watch for them to burn ye out, though. The men in the hay-mow can best see that coming if it does, so mind ye have an ear to 'em. Have ye all an eye to the house. It's ma own flesh and blood in the house. Mind it well.'

'We'll do our best,' Nebraska said with surprising calm. 'There ain't any slackers on the crew. We should be able to have fifteen or twenty men here before Granger can get here. We can hold off a small army with that many good rifles.'

'Aye. That ye can, lad. I'm counting on it. But three of them ye're counting on ye'll not be having. I'll be taking Jake and Bradshaw and Captain Percy with me.'

Nebraska visibly flinched. 'You're right,' he lamented. 'I was countin' on them three real heavy. What's your game?'

'We'll be out of sight where they will most likely be hieing in from,' Ian explained. ' 'Tis the surprise we're counting on. When they think they've us pinned down in house and yard, we'll be finding a spot to cut them to ribbons from the other side. When we open the guns on 'em, I'm betting they run like the yellow rabbits they are.'

Nebraska frowned. 'Then you'll be needing more'n the four of you.'

'Aye. If we can. When men are come from the other ranches, if Granger has not come yet, ye can send at least four more to join us.'

Nebraska nodded. 'Then I need to know where to find you. I'll need to anyway, if I need to get a message to you or ask instructions.'

Ian thought a long moment. 'Aye, lad. 'Tis a reasonable request. We aim to wait in the rocks at the head of that spine that sticks out toward the brae just beyond the spruces yonder. Our horses we can tie in the trees behind and to the left of us, where they'll be out of sight, and we will be watching the approach of the brigands, 'tis near certain. If they use the rise beyond the yard for cover, we'll be right behind them. Captain Percy and Bradshaw will be in the brush around to the east of the buildings, where they can be behind the ones that set up there.'

Nebraska grinned. 'I sure hope I'm where I can

see Granger's face when it happens,' he said. 'Or at least hear 'im cuss.'

' 'Tis my fondest hope ye'll nae hear a word from the rabid skunk,' Ian fired back. ' 'Tis my fondest hope he'll be sent to hell with the first volley. And I'll be askin' God no mercy for his mangy soul.'

'Then let's do it,' Nebraska said. He wheeled and began barking orders as though he had been doing it all his life. By the time Ian, Jake, Snuffy Bradshaw, and the grizzled old Captain Percy rode from the yard, the shutters were already being latched into place and men were approaching their stations.

13

'Listen, lad.'

Ian stood amid the huge boulders at the tip of a hogback, extending outward from the end of a spur of mountain. They were probably 500 yards from the center of the yard, but less than 200 yards behind the low hillock he thought was the most likely place for Granger to set up his gunmen.

Captain Percy and Snuffy Bradshaw had been sent to a vantage point about 120 degrees around an imaginary circle around the ranch. From that point they would be equally able to fire on the rear of a large group of attackers, if they spread out in cover as Ian expected them to. The two fields of fire would nearly converge, so there was little cover they could not rake with their own fire.

'What'd'ya hear?' Jake whispered.

'Horses coming,' Ian whispered back. 'From t'other way, though. It should be for our side.'

A few minutes later they could both hear half a dozen horses thunder into the yard. They could hear Nebraska yell out, 'Glad to see you boys. One man can take the horses to the barn, then join our boys in the hay-mow. One man join the ones in the corral. The other four join the boys in the bunkhouse. Pick a window and look sharp.'

'Rafter R's about half an hour behind us,' they heard an unidentified voice inform Nebraska. 'They'll have a dozen guns when they get here.'

Silence descended on the scene again. Jake could hear scurrying sounds in the timber, as small animals moved about, searching for food. A trout jumped from a pool in the creek, with an unmistakable splash.

'Big trout,' he commented.

'Aye. There are fine fish in the burn. And me with no time to fish for one, even one time this year.'

'Lot o' the year left,' Jake consoled him.

'Aye. If we're living to enjoy it.'

'I plan to,' Jake responded.

The silence returned. A vagrant breeze blew through the spruce and pine timber, emitting a sound like no other in the world. To both men it was as if nature's lullaby had whispered to their souls. As one, they sighed in answer to the wind's sough in the trees. One of their horses blew softly. The bit ring jingled as he scratched the side of his nose against his leg. Closer, a horsefly buzzed in Jake's ear, and he swatted at it. Something like a screen door banged in the yard.

Ten or fifteen minutes of silence returned. Then both men straightened suddenly.

'Now what was that?' Ian queried.

'Two horses,' Jake responded.

'Aye, but going the wrong way, they were. 'Tis out of the yard they went.'

'S'pose Nebraska sent a couple boys somewhere else fer reinforcements?'

'There's no place else to send them, that they could get help and be back in time.'

'Whatd'ya think then?'

'I dunno, lad.'

'Somebody's comin'.'

'Aye. On foot. Running, he is.'

Their eyes were glued to the edge of the trees as Nebraska burst from them, running at top speed. Ian called out to him, speaking softly. 'Ye're waking the dead, Nebraska. What is it?'

'It's Casey,' Nebraska shouted. 'She's gone.'

'Gone?' both men echoed together.

Jake said, 'How could she be gone? She's in the house!'

Nebraska sucked in a couple great gulps of air. 'She was. She went out to the outhouse. She didn't come back. Then two horses took off outa the yard. I went over to the house to check, an' she's gone.'

'What about Lance?' Jake barked.

Nebraska nodded. 'I checked. He's gone too. His horse an' one o' Casey's are missin' from the barn.'

'Now why would the lass be leaving with him?'
Ian wondered aloud. 'And especially with her
knowing he's likely the one that killed Red and
McBirney. And Turnstall too.'

'Not by her choice!' Jake offered. 'He's took her.
I'll ride after 'em.'

'Nay, lad,' Ian argued. ' 'Tis my place. She's my
lassie.'

'And she's the woman I love,' Jake countered.
'And I've got a whole lot more experience than you
do trackin' down scum like Sinclair. I'll have her
and be back before the fireworks are over.'

'I wish I could be that certain,' Ian worried.
' 'Tis the two of us will go, then.'

'No,' Callahan vetoed. 'You're needed here.
Nebraska'll send out another good rifle, maybe
two, to take my place here, more when Rafter R
gets here. I'll be takin' yore horse along, too. Just
so I've got an extra. That'll be better anyhow. They
might hear the horses here an' ruin the surprise.
That or their horses will, an' then yours'll nicker
an answer to 'em.'

Ian sighed heavily. He looked off in several
directions, then nodded. 'Then do ye be goin'.
Bring my lassie back, y'hear?'

'I'll bring her back,' Jake bit the words off as he
moved to the horses. Nebraska rode Ian's horse as
far as the yard, then Jake left the yard at a trot,
leading the extra horse and watching the tracks
left by the departing pair.

He had followed less than a quarter mile when

he began to grin. Look at thet! he marveled. Thet girl's keepin' her horse where there's soft ground every chance she gets. She's leavin' a trail a drunk Indian could foller blindfolded.

He lifted his horse to a gallop, dodging through the branches of the trees. Must have her hands tied to the saddle horn, he observed after a while. She's kickin' a tree when she kin, to bust off a branch, but never with her hands.'

The pace of his following was constantly slowed by the terrain itself. They were keeping well up along the side of the mountain, where there were boulders, small gullies, and intermittent timber. Lance knew where they were going, and set a brisk pace, but Jake couldn't follow at that pace, keep the trail in sight, and still watch for perils that could break a horse's leg or sweep him from the saddle. His frustration began to mount as he realized he was falling further and further behind.

Whenever he had a clear field of view for a ways, he spurred his horse to a run, but had to rein him in again almost immediately when the brief stretch of favorable ground was crossed.

Then he reined in abruptly. The grass was matted down in several places just ahead. He frowned. He looked around warily, and dismounted. Walking forward slowly and carefully, he led his horses, examining the crushed growth minutely.

She fell off her horse! he marveled. Fell plumb off. How'd she manage that?

The sign was unmistakable to his trained eye. The impression in the grass was clear where she had landed. So were the signs that Lance had whirled the horses around, dismounted, and walked to her. He had forced her back on to her horse, and they had ridden on, but not before both sets of tracks walked around a lot more than should have been necessary. He puzzled over the signs, examining every track.

Then he stiffened and moved forward slowly. He could make out scratches in a small area of bare ground, made with the toe of a boot. 'What is thet?' he muttered. 'Looks like a "C", a "T", a "W", an' a crooked line. Why, she'sa tryin' ta tell me somethin'! She knows plumb sure I'll be ridin' after 'er, an' she managed to leave me somethin'. But what's it mean?'

He squatted down, studying the marks carefully. He glanced to the side, and saw where she had been jerked away and propelled toward the horses. He clamped his jaw and forced his attention back to the scratched message.

C, T, W. Now what could that mean?

C, T, W. An' a crooked line. Like a snake. Or maybe a crick, meanderin' along. Crick. Maybe it's where they're goin'. Maybe she got 'im to tell 'er where he's takin' 'er. Crick. Some crick. C, T, W. Catawall. Cottonwall. Cottonwillow. Cottonwood. Cottonwood! Cottonwood Crick! Sure's anythin'. Cottonwood Crick. Lemme think 'bout this now. Cottonwood Crick. I know where thet is. Me'n her went there once, lookin' fer thet bunch o' brindle heifers. The cabin! Thet line shack they keep fer winter. He's takin' her to the line shack to hole up till the fightin's over. But is he tryin' to perteck her from the fightin' or takin' her fer hisself?'

He frowned, forcing his mind to focus. He studied a map in his head of the location of the shack, and the lay of the land between. Then he grinned. 'Bless your heart, girl,' he said. 'You got it figgered out a'ready! Since I know where they're headin', I kin ride cross country, git outa these rocks 'n timber, an' make a whole lot better time than they kin. I oughter be able to be there a-waitin' when they show up.'

He raced to his horse and sprang into the saddle. He guided his mount, with the other horse in tow, at right angles to the trail he had been following. In less than a quarter-mile he emerged from the edge of the timber. The land that stretched out before him was rolling hills and ridges, speckled with sagebrush and soapweeds and grass. He jammed the spurs to his horse's sides. In half a dozen jumps the horses settled into a ground-eating run.

Jake made no effort to stay hidden. He was positive Lance would never expect Casey to be able to get a message to him, or for him to be out of the timber, racing to intercept them. He concentrated on watching for prairie dog or badger holes, and letting his horse run.

Thirty minutes later, he reined in the sweating

mount. He jumped from the saddle and into Ian's saddle, switching the lead rope so he could let his own horse run without his weight. In thirty seconds' time he had switched mounts and was eating up the distance in that smooth running-gait.

Twice more he switched mounts. Each time the mount he switched to was less eager to resume the run, but both horses continued to breathe easily, even though they were breathing heavily and were lathered with sweat.

Emerging from a shallow draw, he spotted the landmark he was looking for. He swung the horses toward a distant neck of timber and allowed them to slow to a swift trot. He studied the trees and rocks intently as he rode. In minutes he could make out the shape of the line shack. It was a small log cabin, set just at the edge of a jutting tongue of timber that thrust out from the darker green of the mountain. He could see no sign of life.

He circled the cabin, keeping well away from the direction he expected Lance and Casey to approach from. He rode on past, finding a thick patch of brush a short distance from a small stream. He swiftly unsaddled both animals. Using one of the saddle blankets, he hurriedly rubbed them both down. By the time he'd finished, they were both busily munching the tall grass. He hobbled both horses, murmuring, 'You fellers ain't gonna wander nowheres, an' you ain't likely to be seen here atwixt the brush an' the crick.'

Moving quickly, he picked out a spot where he could remain hidden and wait.

He had been in place less than half an hour when he heard them coming. He heard Casey first. Her voice was louder than normal, and it puzzled him for a moment. Then he grinned. She knows good'n well I'll be here, he told himself silently. She's makin' sure they don't s'prise me.

'I wish you'd untie my hands from this saddle horn,' Casey complained loudly. 'It's hurting my wrists.'

He could hear Lance mutter something, but could not distinguish the words. He could, however, hear Casey's answer.

'Almost where? Almost to the line shack? Why are we coming here? You know you're going to be in more trouble than you've ever been in your life, don't you? You'd better untie me and let me ride back home.'

They were close enough now for him to hear Lance's response.

'I can't do that, Miss Casey. I can't let you be where there's gonna be all that shootin' an' such. I can't take a chance on you gettin' hurt. Besides, it's time anyway.'

'What's time?' Casey responded. 'Time for what?'

'Time enough fer you to stop bustin' every cowboy's heart in the country an' settle down an' get married.'

'Well, I'm certainly not marrying you!'

'Well, yes, you are, Miss Casey. I done decided. I been in love with you since you was fifteen years old. Do you remember the time I got bucked off'n that big ol' sorrel stud? You helped me up, an' wiped the dirt off'n my face an' all. You sat there on the ground an' held my head on yore lap, an' wiped the dirt an' sweat off my face, till you knowed I was all right. You remember that?'

'I remember it,' Casey affirmed.

'Then when you figgered out I was all right, you up an' got on that ol' stud an' rode 'im plumb inta the ground. You rode him so hard he couldn't buck no more, then you run 'im around that corral till he couldn't do nothin' but stand there all spraddle-legged, his sides a-heavin', breathin' so hard they could hear 'im all over the yard. An' your pa started chewin' ya out fer ridin' 'im that hard, an' you tol' yore pa, "That's what he gets for hurting someone I like". You remember that?'

'I remember it,' she repeated.

'That's when I knowed,' he said.

'Knowed . . . Knew what?'

'That's when I knowed fur plumb sure you was gonna be my woman. My wife. Mrs Lance Sinclair. The only woman in the world for me. That's why I just couldn't never let no one else ever think that maybe they stood a chance with you.'

'You, you killed Red?' Casey asked, forgetting to talk loudly.

It didn't matter any longer. They were close enough for Jake to hear everything they said.

'I didn't have no choice, Miss Casey. He was threatenin' to mess up everything I've planned on since that day when you was fifteen years old. I been watchin' you grow up, and get purtier and purtier every day. An' look more an' more like a woman, till you got to be the best lookin' woman in the whole country. An' I been plannin' on this day fer that whole time.'

'How about Walter?' Casey interrupted. 'Did you kill him, too?'

'Well, what choice did I have?' Lance insisted. 'I saw the way you looked at him, and I sure saw the way he looked at you. Preacher or not, he was runnin' his eyes up an' down all over you the whole time you was sittin' there together.'

'You were watching us?'

' 'Course I was watchin' you! I was always watchin' you. I was watchin' you every time you went ridin' off with that gunfighter, too. He thinks he's some kinda special fighter or somethin'. I follered you every time, an' watched. I pertneart just up an' shot 'im when he kissed you, up there in the aspens. I woulda, too, 'cept that I already figgered this time was comin'. I figgered I could wait till he was away from you, at least. I didn't want you to have to see it happen, you know. I wouldn't do nothin' that'd make you that upset.'

'You tried to kill him, too, didn't you? That was you that shot a hole in his hat a while back!'

'Yeah, that was me. I don't generally miss, that-away. I ain't sure what happened. Musta been a lot further downhill than I figgered. Anyway, Granger's boys'll take care o' him just fine. Well, here we are. This here's our honeymoon cottage, Miss Casey. This here's where we get to become man and wife. You're gonna be so happy, Miss Casey. I been waitin' fer you all my life. I didn't never even go off to the whorehouse when the other hands did, 'cause I was just waitin' fer you.

After all this fightin' is done, we'll ride on back an' tell everyone you're my woman now. We can even get a preacher outa Meeteetse to make the weddin' all proper an' all if you want to. An' if your family's all killed by Granger, we'll be the ones that know what really happened, and we can have him arrested, and get the ranch back, and all.'

'Do you honestly think I'm going to let you . . . to just go along with . . . do you think you can just do whatever you want to do with me?'

'Why, of course I can,' Lance said. His eyes were wide, as if she had said something completely beyond his comprehension. 'Oh, I know I'll likely have to keep you sort of tied up, a little bit. You know, for the first time or two. But you'll see. When you see how much I love you, and what a good husband I can be for you, you'll come around to my way of thinking. You really will. You'll see. Why, after a day or two or three, you'll be loving me just as much as I love you. You'll see.'

He nodded his head emphatically as he said the last 'You'll see'. Then he swung from the saddle and started around his horse toward Casey's mount. As he stepped clear of his horse, Jake moved into the open and barked, 'Hold it right there, Lance! Throw down your gun!'

Lance froze in his tracks. He looked around, frowning in incomprehension.

'Why, Jake! What are you doin' here? You ain't s'posed to be here! You're back at the ranch, waitin' fer Granger an' all them gunfighters.'

'I said, get rid of that gun,' Jake barked. 'Unbuckle that gunbelt and let it drop.'

Lance looked up at Casey, then back at Jake. Carefully, Casey began to nudge her horse, making it sidle away from Lance, putting more distance between herself and her abductor.

Lance shook his head. 'I can't do that! You ain't even s'posed to be here. This here's my weddin' day. Me an' Casey, we're gonna be man an' wife, today. You ain't got no business here.'

'Casey is my business,' Jake disagreed. 'She'll never be yours, Lance. It's all a dream. Now give it up. Get rid of that gun. See, I don't want to hurt you. I haven't even drawn my gun. I don't want to hurt you. I just can't let you hurt Casey. I love her too, Lance. She's my woman, not yours.'

'No!' Lance cried.

With a speed that amazed both Jake and Casey, Lance's gun seemed almost to leap into his hand. It was already spouting fire before it came to bear on Jake. The surprise and the speed of his draw allowed him to get off the first shot. It also caused that shot to go wide, buzzing angrily past Jake's ear. He didn't get the second shot off. Jake's own gun was in his hand, barking three times in rapid succession before Lance could squeeze his trigger again.

Lance was driven backward a step with each bullet that slammed into his chest. Then he stood there, shaking his head slowly back and forth.

'No,' he said softly. 'No. Not this way. Not supposed to be here. My wife.'

He collapsed into a silent and motionless heap. Jake strode forward and kicked his gun well out of his reach, just in case. Then he hurried to Casey. He pulled a knife from its sheath at his belt and sliced through the ropes binding her to the saddle horn. She toppled off the horse into his arms, clinging tightly to him, sobbing suddenly into the security of his shoulder.

14

'Oh, sweetheart, I was never so glad to see anyone in my life. I knew you'd be here. I just knew it. But at the same time I was so afraid you wouldn't see the message I left, or that Lance would have seen it and rubbed it out, or . . .'

Jake stopped the flow of words in the best way he could think of. He pressed his lips against hers. She responded with fervor, whether from relieved fear, or passion, or love, or joy, he really couldn't decide. Then he decided he didn't really care. Whatever it was, it'd be nice to know though, just so he could cause it again.

He pulled away from her, suddenly upset at the confusion his own rising passions were causing in his mind.

'We got to get back,' he said. His voice was unexpectedly hoarse. 'They'll be needin' our guns.'

'They haven't come yet?'

Jake shook his head. 'Hadn't when I left.

Nebraska was sendin' a couple o' the boys with rifles out to join your pa, to take my place, but there wasn't hide nor hair o' Granger yet then. Been a while, though. They could be there by now.'

She nodded. 'I want to see, first.'

'See what?'

'The cabin.'

'The line shack? Why?'

'Lance kept talking about it the whole way. How he'd fixed it up, just for him and me. What all he'd done. The groceries he'd got stocked in. Cleaning. Everything. Talked and talked and talked about it. He kept calling it "our love nest", and all kinds of things. I just wanted to look.'

'Are you sure you want to? Likely he didn't do nothin', 'cept in his mind. He was plumb tetched, ya know.'

She nodded. 'I know. I still want to see.'

Wordlessly he stepped back from her and led the way to the cabin door. He lifted the latch. The two of them stepped in together. They saw nothing for a moment, as their eyes adjusted from the bright sunlight to the dim interior of the cabin. Then Casey gasped. Jake's mouth clamped shut. His lips compressed to a thin line. The muscles bulged on the hinge of his jaw. His fists knotted at his sides, until the knuckles turned white. Casey moved over against him, clinging to his arm. He put an arm protectively around her shoulders.

The cabin was spotlessly clean. It smelled of lye soap and borax. There were no cobwebs, no dust, no lint. It was as spotlessly clean as it could have been made without boiling the entire contents in soapy water. The floor, normally deep with dirt from careless boots, was as clean as the top of a table. Even the stovepipe leading from the pot-bellied stove in the center, to a hole in the roof, had been scrubbed and painted with stove-black.

The shelves along one side were well stocked with food. It was stacked in neatly, with the labels on everything showing, as on a grocery shelf. There was food enough for two people to have lived there for a month or two.

But it was neither the cleanliness nor the food that caught their attention, grabbing their minds and paralyzing them. They both wanted to look away, to turn and leave, to run from there, but they couldn't. They stood, clinging to each other, staring mutely.

At the far side of the room a bed had been arranged on the floor. It was wider than the single bunks that were built into the sides of the cabin. It was the size of a large double bed. Straw or grass had been carefully arranged, then covered with a tarpaulin, folded under neatly so no straw showed. On top of that blankets and a quilt had been tidily arranged. Two pillows, deftly fluffed, lay at the head.

At all four corners of the bed a ring had been secured to the floor. To each ring, the end of a length of soft rope had been securely tied. Then about three feet of that rope was skilfully coiled on top of each corner of the bed.

With a shudder, they both recalled Lance's words. *Oh, I know I'll likely have to keep you sort of tied up, a little bit. You know, for the first time or two. But you'll see. When you see how much I love you, and what a good husband I can be for you, you'll come around to my way of thinking. You really will. You'll see. Why, after a day or two or three, you'll be loving me just as much as I love you. You'll see.*

With a sob, Casey whirled and lunged outside. Jake was half a step behind her. A dozen feet from the front door, she whirled and came back into his arms.

'Oh, Jake! Oh! He really meant it. He really was going to do . . . to do . . . to do all those things to me . . . to tie me to that bed and . . . oh, Jake!'

'I'll burn it,' Jake gritted.

'Burn what?' she sobbed.

'The whole thing! The shack! Burn it to the ground!'

'Oh, don't, Jake. Not the cabin. Papa needs it for a line shack. But drag that bed out here, will you? Do burn it! And those ropes. I want to watch them burn.'

Without a word, Jake turned back to the cabin. He dragged the bedding out to a clear space in a rocky area with little grass. Then he used the tarpaulin to gather and carry the straw and grass that had formed the makeshift mattress. Jake then swept and gathered up every stray straw he could, and piled them all together atop the bedding. He found a jug of coal oil on the shelf, and doused the bedding and straw with it. He lit a corner of it, and stepped back to watch the flames hungrily lick across, enfolding the whole pile in flames.

Casey moved inside the circle of his left arm, trembling. He drew her tightly against him, and side by side they watched the flames consume the nightmare that she had almost been made to live.

The pile of cloth and straw and canvas was reduced to ashes when she said softly, 'Bury him. Please.'

'Who?'

'Lance.'

'Bury him? Why? Leave him to the coyotes.'

She shook her head. 'He was crazy, Jake. But he was human. We can't just let him lie there. We have to bury him. It isn't his fault he went crazy. Enough men have died because of me. I don't want to have to live with thinking of every varmint in the area tearing at his flesh. He was crazy, but he loved me. I really want to bury him.'

Jake thought of several reasons to argue against it, then he shrugged his shoulders instead. He went back into the shack and emerged with a shovel. He walked to the body of the dead cowboy, and began digging a grave right beside where he lay.

It was arduous digging. The ground was hard and rocky. Every time he encountered another rock, he had to dig around it, pry it upward with his shovel, until he could roll it up out of the hole. When he thought the hole was deep enough, he stripped the gun and holster off the dead man and rolled him into the shallow grave. Then he shoveled the dirt back in on top of him and arranged all the rocks in a long cairn on top, to keep any wild animals from digging their way to the body.

Casey stood, hugging herself with her arms, watching wordlessly. When he finished, she walked to him. She put her arms around his waist and looked up into his face. Speaking softly, she simply said, 'Thank you.'

He couldn't think of anything to say; so he kissed her again.

'We'd better go,' she said.

He nodded without speaking. He took the shovel and carefully covered all the remaining coals of the fire with dirt. Then he put the shovel away and carefully secured the door.

'At least it'll be the cleanest line camp any cowboy ever set foot in,' he grinned.

She giggled unexpectedly. Then she laughed. Their pent-up emotions tumbled out in a rush, and they stood there, holding hands, laughing like they'd just heard the funniest joke of their entire lives. They both laughed until the tears ran down their faces.

'Put up a sign,' Casey choked between fits of laughter. '*Take your boots off at the door.*'

Jake nodded his head, trying three times before

he could get words out between his own explosions of laughter, '*And warsh your feet, too. The floor's clean.*'

Just as quickly as it had come, the fit of laughter subsided and faded away. They looked at each other with embarrassment for a moment.

Then he said, 'We'd best go. You take his gun an' holster. I'll poke a couple holes in the belt, so it'll stay on ya. He's got a good rifle.'

He moved Lance's rifle to her saddle scabbard, then adjusted Lance's gunbelt so it would fit her. He fought with all the feelings that welled up within him as he was reaching around her hips, adjusting the leather to fit her.

Abruptly she picked up on the struggle he was having. A mischievous twinkle danced in her eyes.

'Jake Callahan, what are you thinking?' she demanded.

'You don't wanta know,' he growled.

'I want to know exactly what you're thinking.' She repeated the demand.

He straightened and looked into her face. The dancing lights in his own eyes mirrored hers. He drawled, 'I was jist thinkin' it was a plumb mistake to burn up a perfectly good bed without even makin' use of it.'

She slugged him on the shoulder. 'Shame on you! And here I thought you were a gentleman!'

'Now I never ever claimed thet!'

'And a gallant hero.'

'Nor thet.'

'And a man I could trust with my virtue.'

'Yup. Ya kin thet. But you best not trust me with thet body o' yours! I got my limits.'

She giggled and swung into the saddle. 'Where is your horse?'

'I got two,' he replied. 'Mine an' your pa's. I switched mounts back an' forth, so I could run more. They're over by the crick.'

He swung into Lance's saddle, and they rode together after the other two horses. They saddled those animals, for lack of a better way of transporting their gear back with them, and headed back toward the Mill Iron ranch, each leading a horse, riding stirrup to stirrup. From time to time they seemed to respond to the same impulse to look at each other, smile quietly, and sigh heavily.

15

'Moon should be up in another hour,' Jake said.

The brisk trotting of four horses thudded softly. Saddles squeaked. Bit rings jingled. Off to their right, at the edge of the timber, the wings of an owl rustled as it took flight from a tree top.

'How long before we're there?' Casey asked in reply.

' 'Bout the same,' Jake said. 'Maybe an hour.'

'Good. I don't like the idea of riding into the yard without knowing what's going on.'

'Me neither. I don't 'spect we'll ride in anyhow. We'll tie up the horses in thet big draw jist past the little horse-pasture. We'll slip in on foot from there, to figger out what's happenin'.'

'Why aren't we hearing any shooting? Do you think maybe Granger didn't come after all?'

'Not likely. I 'spect they're there. Might be they're jist gettin' there, though. They mighta waited till dark, an' figgered to slip into place afore the moon comes up. Then when the moon makes it light enough, they can commence the festivities.'

Casey giggled. 'That's an odd way of putting it.'

'Didn't know I was all thet eloquent, huh?'

'And just how eloquent are you, my dashing hero?'

'I ain't 'zactly ignorant,' he responded.

'Did you go to school?'

'Yup. I even know how to talk, when it seems worth the effort.'

'And not sound like Texas?' she teased.

With no trace of accent, he said, 'Madam, I can most assuredly inform you that I am capable of being conversant with ladies and gentlemen of high caliber and station, should that occasion arise. Further, please understand I can quote the soliloquy of your choice from *Julius Caesar*.'

She stared at him with open mouth 'I don't believe that! Okay, mister scholar, quote me Anthony's speech.'

As though addressing a theater audience he began: 'Friends, Romans, countrymen, lend me your ears. I come to bury Caesar, not to praise him. The evil that men do lives after them. The good is oft interred with their bones. So let it be with Caesar . . .'

'I'm impressed,' she interrupted him. 'Where did you learn that?'

'In school, of course. Jist 'cause I'm from Texas, don't mean I ain't got no schoolin'.'

'Then why on earth do you talk like, like, you're illiterate?'

'Why not? Thet's the way most folks talk, where I come from. If'n I talk like a schoolmarm, they'll all figger I'm puttin' on airs an' such. Man don't make many friends tryin' ta impress folks.'

'Why, Jake Callahan, you are a most amazing man!'

' 'Course I am,' he responded at once. 'I gotta be. You wouldn't go fallin' in love with jist anybody, would you?'

The night was too dark, even with the brightness of the stars, to see if his eyes were dancing, but she was confident they were. She started to answer when he spoke again.

'I 'spect we'd best cut the chatter now. 'Nother half-mile we'll slow down to a walk, an' move kinda quiet-like. After we tie up the horses, we'll hafta not talk atall.'

'There won't be any of Granger's men clear around on this side, will there?'

'I ain't sure. They shouldn't be. But if'n they come with forty or fifty men, figgerin' we're gonna be all set up fer 'em, they may try to get fellers all the way around the place. Figgerin' they'd just come quick an' straight away, your pa jist set up fellers to be behind 'em on the other side. But since they ain't started nothin' yet, they's most likely sendin' someone around ta this side too. They'll have ta go the long way around, ta git ta this side without bein' seen. That may be why they ain't started nothin' yet. We'd sure hear shootin' by now, if they'd started anythin'.'

They rode in silence then, with only the squeaking of their saddles marking their descent into the draw. They hurriedly tied the horses to trees along the edge of the draw. Carrying their rifles and the extra ammunition from the saddle-bags, and each wearing a pistol, they looked at each other and nodded. Jake led the way, with Casey following right behind.

They skirted the edge of the horse pasture, watching, listening carefully. Every few steps, Jake would stop and stand perfectly still for a moment, listening, then proceed.

They were nearly to an outcrop of rocks when a soft voice carried to his ear. He crouched, motioning Casey to do the same. They remained motionless, listening.

In a few minutes, they heard it again. Two men were talking softly, a-ways ahead of them. In a few minutes they could hear the shuffling of feet, and the rustling of clothing against rock from several places.

Jake frowned. He delved into his mind for the details of the way the land lay on this side of the ranch yard. He had only been in this area once, and that was just for a quick look around. Like most of his breed, however, once he had seen a place he could recall it in almost perfect detail.

Nodding, finally, he motioned to Casey. Moving off at an oblique angle, they began to climb the

side of a hill. At the top of the low rise, huge
jagged rocks thrust up through the earth, making
a jumble of square-shouldered boulders it was
nearly impossible to walk through.

Moving slowly and silently, he slipped around
the front of that outcropping. At the lower end of
it, but still considerably higher than the terrain in
front of them, smaller rocks and boulders were
strewn as if by some giant hand. He picked a
place near the outer edge of those, which gave
them both a clear field of fire in front, and the
protection of the rocks. They each had a niche to
shoot through that would present an almost
impossible target to anyone shooting back.

They settled into place and he glanced at the
eastern sky. A tiny sliver of moon was just begin-
ning to appear.

'Perfect timin',' he gloated silently.

Within fifteen minutes, it was as if daylight had
dawned. Without the harshness of the sun, the
land was bathed in the soft, almost ethereal light
of the full moon. Accustomed to the darkness as
their eyes were, it was almost as good as daylight
to see around.

Directly in front of them, perhaps 500 yards,
the ranch yard of the Mill Iron lay spread to view.
The moon was so bright Jake could make out
brands on the horses in one of the corrals.

'Musta had too many fellers show up to help, to
be able to keep the horses in the barn!' he realized. 'They must have fifty or sixty guns in there.'

Between them and the yard, scattered among the trees and brush, most no more than fifty yards in front of them they could see at least six men. Some were lying prone behind fallen logs. A couple were kneeling behind trees. Some had found large rocks to crouch behind. They appeared to be waiting for some sort of signal. One of them raised his head and surveyed the ranch yard. He recognized the same thing Jake had noticed.

'Look at all them horses!' one of them whispered.

'They's half a dozen different brands I kin see from here,' another one responded, craning his neck.

'They figgered out we was comin'! They called in help,' a third voice concurred.

'Ain't gonna help 'em none,' a fourth voice opined.

'Gonna make 'em hard to smoke out.'

'Not when Granger cuts loose with thet cannon, it ain't.'

'You boys be ready,' a different voice ordered. 'When thet first cannon shot fires, an' a whole wall o' the house falls down, they's gonna be scared rabbits runnin' all over thet yard. Be ready to mow 'em down as soon as they break cover.'

Casey looked at Jake, her eyes wide with fright. Jake frowned. They were in no position to do anything other than hope. If Ian or the others staked out in the rocks and trees had spotted the cannon, they might have already taken it out of the picture.

If not . . . well, they'd have to wait and see.

Jake shrugged his shoulders, unable to offer Casey any consolation. He saw a shudder run through her body, but no other indication of her thoughts.

They had no more time to worry, The roar of a cannon shook the ground and hammered at their ears. Several of the men in the rocks below them cursed.

An ear-splitting crash issued from the far side of the ranch house. Someone inside the house screamed. A man cursed.

Several men ran into the yard from the barn and the corrals. As soon as they appeared, the men in front and below Jake and Casey began to rake the yard with rifle fire. In seconds, two men were down in the yard. The rest dropped to the earth and began trying to return the fire.

Neither Jake nor Casey spoke. They let their rifles do it for them. Their first shots were fired in almost perfect unison. One man yelled as a bullet plowed through his back and out his chest, then he fell forward across the rock he had been using as cover. The other man made no sound at all. He was prone behind a log, firing over the top of it. His head dropped onto the log. His rifle slipped from his fingers. He did not move.

Their second shots were just as effective, and in less than five seconds four of the gunmen were taken out of the battle. With those shots, someone realized they were being fired on from behind.

'There's someone behind us!' he bellowed.

As he yelled, he leaped to his feet, firing wildly in the direction the shots were coming from. Then he threw his hands in the air. His rifle went flying behind him and to his right. He stood there, arms spread upward, for a full heartbeat, then toppled backward and lay still.

Another man broke from his cover and began to run. He was cut down in mid-stride by a snap shot from Casey's rifle.

A man neither of them had seen stood up from the tall grass and began cursing furiously and firing in their direction. A shot from the yard entered the base of his skull and exited through his nose, taking his fear, his anger, and his life, scattering them together into the brush and grass. He died before he could even know he had been hit.

Just then a massive explosion shook the earth. Men screamed and yelled. A ball of fire lifted through the trees on the other side of the ranch yard, shooting more than a hundred feet into the air. In the light of that ball of fire pieces of debris could be seen soaring off in all directions.

'What was that?' Jake said aloud.

Casey's giggle sounded ridiculous and out of place.

'Papa found the cannon,' she said with total certainty. 'He blew up their barrel of powder.'

It took a moment for her words to register. He wanted to argue.

'How do you know that?' he wanted to demand. But he couldn't think of any alternative explanation.

16

Ian and two hands from the Rafter R crouched silently in the rocks. As the moon came up, the whole scene was bathed with soft light. Then they watched with growing satisfaction as more than a dozen men crept into place along the ridge separating the ranch yard from the timber beyond. Unaware of the men hiding behind them, the gunmen stationed themselves where they could fire on the ranch yard from relative safety. They had no idea that their flank was clearly exposed to fire from the men in the rocks.

The two men with Ian stayed perfectly silent and waited for his orders. Their frowns deepened as they waited, however. Time passed slowly. They looked at each other in mute sharing of confusion. Why didn't they start? Why was nobody shooting? What were they waiting for?

Then, from up the mountain behind them, they heard strange noises. Talking in hoarse whispers and grunting, men could be heard doing something. What they were doing, Ian couldn't imagine.

Then silence descended again. The silence was shattered minutes later by a hideous roar from behind them, high on the hill at whose tip they hid and waited. The ground trembled beneath them. An instant later, a grinding crash sounded from the ranch house, as though some huge boulder had crashed into the logs, shattering them. Ian and the other two men stared at each other in mute confusion for an instant. Then Ian whispered:

'Cannon! They fetched in a cannon! They're firin' on ma house with a cannon!'

The others stared back, open-mouthed. The gunmen who were spread out in front of them began a steady and rhythmic fire into the ranch buildings.

Ian whispered, 'Stay as ye be. In two minutes, then ye can take out everyone in sight of ye.'

Without waiting for an answer he whirled and began climbing the hill behind him. Moving with surprising speed and agility, he flitted like a shadow from rock to rock, tree to tree. He forced himself to breathe steadily, quietly.

As the hill leveled off at the top there was a little clearing. In the clearing a small cannon was set up. Two men were busily reloading it. Walter Granger stood just beyond it, a smug expression on his face.

Just behind and to the near side of the cannon,

two barrels of gunpowder stood. One of them was open. A measure lay on top of the powder, having been replaced after the measured amount of powder was loaded into the cannon.

Ian moved to a spot behind the largest tree he could see. Holding his rifle against the side of the trunk, he sighted carefully, aiming at the closed barrel of gunpowder. He squeezed the trigger.

He never heard the report of his rifle. Instead, the hammer fell on the loudest explosion he had ever heard. The bullet entered the barrel of gunpowder, sparking as it penetrated a stave, setting the powder off. It instantly set off the barrel beside it by its concussion. A huge ball of fire rocketed into the air, out of Ian's sight. The three men closest to it, including Walter Granger, were killed instantly without even knowing what had happened. Beyond them, three other men went down screaming, with wounds and burns that would prove fatal within minutes.

'Fire a cannon at my house, will ye?' Ian gritted. Then he turned and climbed back down to rejoin the men he had left.

Gunshots followed the explosion from half a dozen places around the yard. Shouts and curses were springing up from everywhere, as the hidden men on the attackers' flanks began riddling their ranks with careful and steady fire. Through the din and confusion, Jake and Casey could clearly hear several voices offering to surrender and pleading for mercy.

Then the booming voice of Ian McFee silenced the growing frenzy.

'Listen to me, lads!' he called out. 'Listen well. I'll be saying it once.'

At the sound of his voice, Casey exclaimed, 'Oh! Thank God! Papa's all right!'

The voices dwindled and died. An unnatural hush descended. Into that hush, Ian's voice carried even to where Jake and Casey remained hidden, so they could understand him clearly, even though they couldn't see him.

'Walter Granger is gone to hell in little pieces and bits. 'Tis where the man belongs,' Ian shouted. 'Him and the cursed cannon he brought to ma ranch with him. We've blown the two of them to kingdom come together, that's what we've done. Ye've nobody left to pay your wages. The sheriff is on his way. I'm a kind man, and I'm not wishing evil on ye. Those of ye what can still stand and walk, can come into the yard with your hands in the air. Ye'll be relieved of your weapons, and we'll be lettin' ye leave. If yui're still here when the sheriff arrives, ye'll be dealin' with him instead o' me, and 'tis likely he'll hang the lot of ye. Now, if yui're wantin' to walk away from here among the livin', 'tis time to walk into the yard with your hands in the air.'

Silence returned. It seemed to seep into the rocks and trees. It shrouded the ranch buildings. It wrapped itself in stifling folds around those who waited and listened. Then it was ripped asunder and disappeared at the voice of one man.

'I'm comin' in. Don't shoot.'

Almost immediately a gunman stood from behind a boulder. Hands in the air, he walked into the yard.

Another hushed silence descended, as those still in hiding waited to see what would happen. When nothing did, another voice said, 'Me too. Don't shoot.'

It was as if a flood-gate opened then. A chorus of voices all saying the same thing rose from a circle around the ranch yard. Every voice was followed by a man rising from hiding, thrusting his hands in the air, and walking into the yard. Within minutes the yard seemed filled with frightened men standing in an almost perfect circle, all with their hands sticking up like pickets of a stockade.

From directly in front of Jake and Casey, then from off to their right, four men stood, called out to the yard, then began to walk.

'I never saw two of them at all,' Casey breathed.

'I knowed all but one was there. I hadn't spotted him,' Jake agreed.

Ian strode into the yard. He started barking orders, bringing order to the milling confusion. In minutes, a stack of weapons had been made. Two hands had been sent out with one of the surrendered gunmen, to retrieve the horses from where the marauders had hidden them. The prisoners were all herded into one part of the yard, where they were surrounded and guarded by Mill Iron hands and those who had come to help them.

As soon as the horses were brought in, four other teams were made up, each comprising two Mill Iron hands and one prisoner. Each team was sent out to the perimeter of the yard to find and retrieve the bodies of those who had been killed. Rather than join the confusion in the yard, Jake and Casey climbed atop one of the large, square-shouldered boulders. They seemed to themselves to be observers, watching some strange dream unfold before them. They sat there, cuddled close to one another, watching and listening. As the team of searchers drew close, Jake said softly:

'There's five of 'em right down here.'

At the first word, Nebraska cursed and whirled, his gun coming to bear on them. He recognized them instantly, and lowered the gun.

'Dang you, Jake! I mighta killed you!'

'Jist fer a second, I thought you was gonna,' Jake agreed. Then he repeated, 'They's five of 'em right out here in front of us.'

Nebraska studied them both.

'Five of 'em. You two accounted for yourselves right well.'

Casey said nothing. She just laid her head over against Jake's shoulder.

'Yup,' Jake said simply.

'You found Casey, I see.'

'Yup.'

'You OK, Miss Casey?' he queried.

'Yup,' Jake answered for her. 'She's a little shook, but plumb fine.'

'You find Lance?'

'Yup.'

'Bring 'im back?'

'Nope.'

'What'd ya do with 'im?'

'Buried him over by the Cottonwood Crick line shack.'

Nebraska digested the information silently, chewing it over in his mind for a long moment.

'Sorta lost 'is mind, didn't he?'

Jake sighed. 'Yup,' he said. 'Sorta lost mine, too.'

'What? You did? How's that?'

'Well, I allays said any man that'd fall in love with a woman had ta be crazy. Guess I lost my mind too.'

Casey elbowed him in the ribs. Nebraska just grinned, and turned to the other two members of his team.

'You boys get these men heaved up onto their saddles.'

He turned back to Jake and Casey. 'You two headin' fer the yard directly?'

Casey said, 'I'm too tired to move.'

Nebraska looked inquiringly at Jake. Jake sighed.

'I know,' Nebraska said, 'but your pa's worryin' about ya somethin' fierce. We gotta go let him know you're OK.'

Jake nodded. 'We was plumb glad ta hear him

sing out thataway. We didn't know but what he'd been spotted in them rocks an' picked off, till then.'

'Sure took care o' that cannon, didn't he?'

Jake grinned. 'I never seen nothin' like thet in my whole life. I could feel the ground shake, clear over here. I bet Ian can't hear nothin', if he was the one close to it when it blew up.'

'He was,' Nebraska affirmed. 'When they shot it the first time, he figured out it was only a hundred yards above him, on the same hill. He slipped up through the trees and shot the powder barrel they brought to load it with. Two barrels. They both went up. Granger was blowed plumb to pieces, along with two of his hands.'

'Serves 'em right,' Jake gritted.

'Where's your horses?' Nebraska thought to ask.

'They're tied in the draw just past the horse pasture,' Jake said. 'If you'd send someone after 'em, I'd sure be obliged. Me'n Casey'll walk over ta the yard.'

'Three horses?' Nebraska asked.

'Four,' Jake corrected. 'I took mine an' Ian's both when I rode after 'em.'

Nebraska nodded wordlessly and turned back to the gruesome chore before him.

Jake jumped off the rock and held up his arms to Casey. She slid off, into his embrace. He held her there for a long moment, then turned. Together they headed for the yard, and a future neither had dared to dream.